SEBASTIAN THE TROUBLEMAKER

CHARLES HENDRICK

Published by Acorn Independent Press Ltd, 2015.

ISBN 978-1-909121-94-2

Acorn Independent Press

CHAPTER 1

Sebastian rubbed his sleepy eyes and slowly made his way over to his bedroom window. Early morning sunlight flooded the room as he opened the blinds and peered out across the sprawling cityscape of tiled rooftops and small, private squares. Looking down, Sebastian noticed that his father's car was still parked in the driveway.

"*He hasn't left yet!*" he thought.

Sebastian's father, Mr Howard, usually went to the office at his factory several times each week, and occasionally he would take his son with him. It had been seven weeks since Sebastian's last visit, and he hoped he might be allowed to go today. The factory was an asphalt plant that was situated on the outskirts of the city, and it provided the family's main source of income. As the owner and director, Mr Howard didn't work regular hours at the plant like his employees, preferring instead to spend much of his time managing the commercial side of his business from the comfort of his home.

Sebastian got dressed quickly, grabbed his watch off the bedside cabinet and then combed his hair to the side. Feeling giddy, he slid down the banisters and ran into the kitchen. His father was sitting at the table, flicking through the morning newspapers, and his mother was cooking breakfast. The couple were chatting yet again about a government regime change that had recently occurred. One of the country's major political parties had seized power via a coup, and for the last few days it had been the main topic of conversation on the lips of almost every adult Sebastian knew. However, he was getting tired of hearing about it, for, at nine years old, Sebastian had little interest in politics. And besides, life in the nation had barely changed since the new party had come to power.

"Good morning," his parents said in unison as their son walked into the room.

Sebastian returned the greeting and took his place at the kitchen table.

"How are you feeling this morning?" Mrs Howard asked.

"Good. I'm feeling much better today," he replied.

Sebastian had had his appendix removed two weeks earlier and was still recovering from the operation. It was now Friday, and he was due to return to school on Monday.

Sebastian stared across the table, looking at his father intently. "So, we agreed that I can come with you to the manufacturing plant today, didn't we?" he said in a pleading voice.

Mr Howard had not in fact agreed to his son's request, but Sebastian decided to try his luck. Mr Howard looked over at his son and squinted through his spectacles. "You're not well enough to go to school today, but you're well enough to come with me to the plant?" he asked with a frown, looking up from the stocks and shares page of his newspaper.

"Oh, let him go!" Mrs Howard said.

"Alright, alright..." Sebastian's father replied casually.

A little smile appeared across Sebastian's lips.

Mrs Howard began serving breakfast, which consisted of eggs, bacon, beans, sausages, black pudding, fried mushrooms, tomatoes, and toast. The family chatted while they ate, and Sebastian's mother mentioned that one of their neighbours had recently had a sunroom extension fitted.

"I wonder how much they paid for it," Sebastian's father immediately said.

"I'm not sure, but I expect it was quite expensive," his wife replied.

"I saw a fox in the garden last night," Sebastian said, trying to change the topic of conversation to something more interesting.

"Oh?" his mother asked.

He was about to elaborate when his father blurted out, "Do you think we should get a sunroom extension?"

"Oh I don't mind, whatever you want dear," Mrs Howard replied as she stirred a pot of tea.

Sebastian just shrugged his shoulders. Mr Howard then looked at his watch.

"My word, it that the time? We'd better get going," he said, giving Sebastian a nod.

As Mrs Howard loaded the used plates and cutlery into the dishwasher, the pair thanked her for the delicious breakfast and then headed out into the hallway.

"Have fun, but be careful!" she said.

Stopping to look at himself in the large antique hall mirror, Sebastian wiped a small spot of brown dirt from his nose and then leant down and gave his shoes a quick polish.

He and his father made their way out through the front door of their period detached house and out onto the gravelled driveway. They climbed into Mr Howard's shiny black Jaguar and put on their seatbelts. Mr Howard slowly reversed out and onto the road. It was a quiet morning in the leafy suburbs with little traffic. The sun shone intensely in the clear blue sky, which was mottled only by a few light clouds. Sebastian yawned and stretched his hands above his head.

"I wonder if we will catch any slackers today?" he asked, turning to his father. He always found it funny when he and his father showed up at the plant unannounced and caught workers slacking on the job. They were quickly sent back to work.

"We'll have to wait and see," Mr Howard replied as he pressed down slightly on the accelerator.

After about 25 minutes driving, the environment was becoming more and more desolate as the cityscape faded away. Through the morning haze, Sebastian could see the outline of electricity pylons and enormous factory buildings in the distance. Tall chimneystacks sprouted from the factory rooftops, billowing columns of thick grey smoke up into the sky. They were getting close now. Mr Howard took a turn off the main road and drove down a narrow roadway until they reached a wire fence. Two men wearing yellow hard hats opened the metal gate and gave a nod as the car drove on through. Mr Howard parked near four big metal silos at the front of the plant. As they opened the doors to get out, the strong smell of molten asphalt filled

Sebastian's nostrils. Clouds of dust hung in the air as the plant employees went about their work, and lorries and trucks manoeuvred about on the large forecourt. Sebastian and his father walked past several thick metal pipes and a conveyer. The sun was shining brightly, and on several occasions the glint on the plant's metallic structures caused Sebastian to look away.

They made their way up a short flight of steel steps into one of the plant's corrugated buildings. As they walked along the corridors, the workers smiled at Sebastian and said hello. Mr Howard sometimes stopped to talk to members of his staff, discussing matters concerning productivity, finances, etc. When Sebastian and his father entered the director's office, they were greeted by the sight of a group of men casually lounging around, drinking cups of coffee and having a chat. One of them was even sitting in Mr Howard's chair and had his feet up on the desk! Mr Howard looked at his watch and tapped the glass. "Working hard?" he asked, giving them a stark look.

Sebastian pulled up his shirtsleeve and stared at his watch, mimicking his father. The men immediately put down their cups and got back to work. Sebastian gave a little chuckle.

As Mr Howard was looking at some graphs pinned to the office wall, two individuals, a man and a woman, appeared as if from nowhere. The man had a thick black moustache and wore a suit and tie, and the woman was small and chubby and wore a grey skirt and jacket. Sebastian noticed that his father seemed slightly agitated as the pair began chatting to him.

"We will each need a hard hat," the woman said.

Mr Howard immediately obliged and picked up two hats that were hanging on hooks on the wall. After he had fitted and adjusted his hat, the man with the moustache looked down at Sebastian and gave him a friendly pat on the head and tousled his hair. Sebastian beamed a cheerful smile.

Mr Howard led the duo around the plant, stopping every few seconds to look at various pieces of machinery. Sebastian discretely tagged along behind the trio, keeping a good distance back so as not to appear ill-mannered. The woman kept asking Sebastian's father questions while her companion jotted down his answers on a writing pad attached to a clipboard. After about an hour they had circumnavigated the entire plant and ended up back at the director's office where they had started. Mr Howard asked his son to wait on the factory floor while he held a meeting with the couple and closed the door. Sebastian felt a bit exhausted from all the walking, so he put his hands in his pockets and leaned back against the wall.

Some plant workers cautiously walked towards him and gathered round. They all had big smiles on their faces and told Sebastian that they had heard wonderful things about him from his father. They asked him why he wasn't at school, and he told them about his recent appendectomy.

"Was it sore?" one of the men asked.

"Yes, for about a week after the operation," Sebastian told him. They then asked about his hobbies and interests, and how school was going. Sebastian told them that he had a keen interest in science and that he liked school.

"And who are that man and woman your daddy's talking to?" one of them asked.

"I don't know," Sebastian replied truthfully.

The workmen continued chatting with Sebastian for a few more minutes, asking him about the games he liked to play and the cartoons he watched on television. Eventually the office door opened and Mr Howard, the moustachioed man and the chubby woman walked out. The workmen who were talking to Sebastian quickly scattered. After Mr Howard had shown the pair out, he called over to his son and said that they'd better get going.

Sebastian waved goodbye to the workers as his father and he left the building and headed back to the car. As they drove home, Sebastian asked his father about the two individuals who had visited him that day.

"Oh, that lady and gentleman just wanted to talk to me about some health and safety procedures at the plant, but it's nothing to worry about," Mr Howard said reassuringly.

That evening after dinner, Sebastian dusted some oil paintings on the living room walls and then practised pieces of music on the family's Broadwood piano.

Before he knew it, it was eight o'clock and time for bed. Sebastian made his way up to his room and glanced briefly out of his bedroom window at the glowing city skyline. Then he closed the blinds, got undressed and hopped into bed. As he drew the blankets over him, he could hear his parents ascending the creaky stairs.

"Will you read me a bedtime story?" he shouted out in as pleading a tone as he could muster.

"Not this again, Sebastian" Mr Howard said as the couple entered his room. "You're almost 10. Aren't you getting a bit old for bedtime stories?"

"Ahh, don't be such a grump," Mrs Howard said looking at her husband.

"Oh fine then..." Sebastian's father replied with a slight sigh. Mrs Howard took a book of bedtime stories out of a drawer in the cabinet beside Sebastian's bed and his father dimmed the lights.

The couple then sat down at the end of their son's bed and began to read one of the stories. It was called *Hansel and Gretel.* Mr and Mrs Howard respectively read out the male and female dialogue. The tale was about a brother and sister who are abandoned in the woods by their father and evil stepmother. A wicked witch who plans to eat them eventually kidnaps them! Sebastian's eyes opened wide and he slowly pulled the fine linen bed-sheets up over his mouth as the horrifying thought of the witch cannibalising the poor children ran through his mind. Thankfully she doesn't get to eat them though. The children kill the witch and find their way back home where they live happily ever after with their father (their evil stepmother had died during their absence).

At the end of the story Sebastian cheered, delighted that the children had made it home safely; although he did feel a twinge of sadness because the witch and stepmother had died.

But now it was time for Sebastian to go to sleep. Mrs Howard placed the book of bedtime stories back in the bedside cabinet's drawer and her husband turned off the light.

"Sweet dreams," they said, kissing him goodnight, and then they closed the bedroom door after them.

* * *

The next morning, Sebastian went to the supermarket with his mother and helped her with the shopping. In the afternoon and evening, he lent a hand as his father did some DIY around the house. As their house was more than a century old, it would occasionally require some handiwork to keep it in good order.

* * *

On Sunday, Sebastian went round to his best friend Adam's house, which was just a few doors down from his own. Adam was a small boy with an unruly mop of blond hair, which he habitually brushed out of his eyes every few seconds. He had the look of a mad scientist and the personality to match. The boys had known each other for most of their lives as their parents were good friends and they were also in the same class at school.

"Where are your parents?" Sebastian asked, noticing that the house was unusually quiet as they lay on the drawing room carpet playing with some tin soldiers.

"They're at the races, but my grandmother is upstairs," Adam replied. "One of father's horses is having his first race today and they wanted to be there to watch." He pointed to some framed photographs, sitting on a decorative chest of drawers. "He's the one being ridden by the jockey dressed in yellow. His name is Hayek."

Aware that Sebastian wasn't particularly interested in horseracing, Adam asked him if he wanted to see the tree house that he was constructing.

"Oh yes please!" Sebastian replied enthusiastically.

Adam led Sebastian out through the back door and to a huge oak tree at the end of the garden. He climbed up a rope ladder attached to the tree and got to work, hammering nails into the wooden tree house, while Sebastian sent him up supplies in a basket via a system of pulleys and ropes. They worked on the project for some time, and when they'd had enough, they made their way into Adam's house for a well-earned rest. Adam's parents arrived home from the races soon afterwards.

The couple looked very formal, even by their own standard. Mr Smith wore a grey tweed suit and waistcoat, and his wife a pink dress and pearl necklace. Adam immediately asked how Hayek had done in his race, and they said that he had finished fourth.

"Well, that's not bad for a first race," Sebastian said, trying to put a good spin on the outcome.

"Ah, young Sebastian!" Mr Smith exclaimed, only now noticing his presence.

He first asked after Sebastian's mother and father and then began to ask questions about the family's asphalt plant. Whenever Sebastian spoke with Mr Smith he always enquired about the plant, for he was an entrepreneur and his conversation invariably revolved around business-related matters. In fact, he rarely talked about anything else, except his beloved horses.

Sebastian told him that he and his father had visited the plant two days previously and had caught some workers resting in the director's office.

"Typical!" Mr Smith said, throwing his head back in laughter. "I hope your father fired them?"

Sebastian paused for a second, "Well no, he just sent them back to work."

"Ah, I see…" Mr Smith replied, looking a little disappointed. Sebastian then politely listened as Adam's father ranted about how lazy employees could be and how they needed to be kept in check at all times.

"I think the boys want to play now," Mrs Smith said to her husband, as she walked in through the drawing room door carrying a plate of cookies. After she placed the plate down on an antique mahogany table, she nudged Mr Smith gently in his ribs and led him out of the room. The boys played a game of Trivial Pursuit to while away the afternoon. Eventually, Sebastian began to grow hungry and said he'd better get home for his dinner.

"See you tomorrow at school," Adam said to him as he left.

Back at his own house, his mother was in the kitchen preparing roast pheasant while his father was in the dining room setting the table with the family's fine bone china, silverware and linen napkins. Sebastian put on a CD of classical music, which the family enjoyed listening to as they ate Sunday dinner. Mrs Howard served the food, and after Sebastian had said grace, they began to eat.

Mr Howard asked his son if he'd spoken to Mr Smith while he was over at Adam's house, and Sebastian confirmed that he had. "Did he mention anything about investment opportunities?" he asked as he poured himself a glass of wine. But Sebastian said that he couldn't remember as he had eventually tuned out as Mr Smith rambled on. "You should really pay more attention when Adam's father talks about business matters," Mr Howard said as he sipped his drink. "All that knowledge will be beneficial to you when you're older."

* * *

The following morning, Sebastian's mother had to call him three times before he finally got out of bed. He stumbled around his room drowsily as he put on his school uniform, and then threw his schoolbag over his shoulder. When he finally arrived downstairs, it was too late for breakfast. Mrs Howard handed him his jacket and ushered him towards the front door. "You're going to be late!" she repeated over and over.

Sebastian waved to his father, who was sitting at the computer in the living room, looking through some spreadsheets related to his asphalt plant. "Have a good day at school," he responded, his eyes barely moving off the screen.

Sebastian made his way along the footpath, idly skimming his hand along the black iron railings that ran the length of his street.

"Wait for me Sebastian!" a voice yelled. He turned around to see Adam cycling in his direction. He was wobbling back and forth on his bicycle as he strained to see through his thick blond fringe. When he caught up with Sebastian, he dismounted and wheeled his bicycle along so he could chat to his friend as they continued their journey together through the cherry-blossom-lined suburban streets. After 15 minutes, they reached the tall, ornate school gates.

They made their way up the winding school avenue, giving a wave to the elderly gardener who was panting heavily as he pushed his petrol-powered lawnmower across the manicured lawns. The large redbrick school building was speckled with patches of lichen and ivy, and magpies fluttered about near one of its chimneys. Sebastian and Adam walked into the airy entrance hall where some fellow students were hurriedly completing homework assignments before classes started.

Black and white photographs of former headmasters adorned the walls, and a faded etching of a man wearing a white, powdered wig hung above the hall's marble fireplace. Students bantered as they proceeded in an orderly procession up the building's solid oak staircase. Glass cases containing numerous awards that the school and its students had won throughout the years were placed at various points along the stairwell.

Adam and Sebastian made their way to their classroom, which was in room number 3. Geographical maps and a periodic table hung from the walls, and the students' wooden desks contained inkwells; a testament to the age of the school. It seemed that it was a full class today; almost everyone was present – David, William, George, Michael, Theresa, Eric, Iain, Maria, Christopher, Eleanor, Jeremy and so on. The students chatted quietly while waiting for class to start. When Mr Stevens walked in, all the children went silent and stood up. Mr Stevens was Sebastian's favourite teacher. He was also the school's headmaster, and divided his time between teaching literature and administrative duties. He was in his late 40s or early 50s and had a hint of grey in his brown hair. As always, he was wearing a pinstriped suit with a purple and yellow tie under his black academic gown.

"Welcome back to school, Sebastian," he said as he gestured to the class to sit back down. "Now children, before we start today's lessons—"

"Sorry I'm late sir," Sayeeda interrupted as she hurried in through the classroom door, quickly loosening her scarf and taking her seat.

Mr Stevens gave her a fleeting look and then continued. "It has come to my attention that one of you has been harassing ducks at the local park!" The students began to look around at each other, wondering who the guilty party could be. "Would anybody like to own up to the offence?" the headmaster asked, his eyes scouring the room.

Slowly, one by one, the children began to look towards a boy sitting at the back of the class. His name was Michael, or "Mischievous Michael" as Mr Stevens called him. He had sandy hair, chubby cheeks, and a sassy smile permanently etched on his face.

"Well Michael, have you anything to say?" Mr Stevens asked.

"It was me," Michael replied sheepishly, staring down at his desk.

"I might turn a blind eye to a bit of high jinks every now and then, but what I won't stand for is unnecessary cruelty to ducks," the headmaster declared with a quiver of anger in his voice. "You're on thin ice, Michael," he added, pointing his index finger directly at the unruly student.

Mr Stevens told everyone to take out their books as it was time to do some reading. The book that the class was currently working from was *Fairy Tales* by the Danish author Hans Christian Andersen. The headmaster asked David to read one of the stories out to the class. David was head boy at the school. He was a tall boy who was considered one of the smartest children in the class and also an excellent sportsman.

The story in question was called *The Emperor's New Clothes*. It was about a vain emperor who is tricked by two tailors into believing that they have created a new suit of clothes for him. The tailors tell the emperor that the clothes are exquisite, but that stupid people can't see them. In reality there are no new clothes, but not wanting to appear stupid, the emperor pretends that he can see them. When he appears naked in public, all the townsfolk profess that they can see the beautiful new clothes, lest they be considered simpleminded. Eventually, a little boy cries out. "Look! The emperor has got nothing on!" Everybody then burst into laughter and admits that they too could see him naked. The emperor feels very embarrassed as he realises that the townsfolk are right. However, he nonetheless pretends that he is wearing clothes and continues on with the procession.

When David had finished reading, the class giggled at the amusing story. Mr Stevens cast his gaze over the room and he and Sebastian locked eyes. "Sebastian, would you please tell us what is the moral of this story?" he asked.

Sebastian thought for a few seconds, summing up the story in his mind before answering. "The moral is to make up your own mind about things, and not just mindlessly go along with the crowd."

"Yes. Very good" Mr Stevens replied. "In other words, always make sure to think for yourself, and if you believe something is wrong, speak up."

Mr Stevens asked everyone to turn over the page to the next story, which was called *The Ugly Duckling*. "You might appreciate this one Michael," Mr Stevens said, staring towards the back of the class. "Maybe you could read it out to us?"

All the boys and girls in the class laughed at Mr Stevens' witticism.

"There once was an ugly duckling…" Michael began. The class continued reading and critically evaluating other fairy tales. Whenever the moral of a story was ambiguous, Mr Stevens would encourage his students to engage in lively debate.

After Mr Steven's class, the students sat through maths and science lessons (taught by teachers Mr Nuttall and Mr Whittaker respectively). As with most school days, the time passed relatively slowly for the children. Their curriculum was broad, and in addition to the core subjects, the children also studied Latin and Classics Allowing for the fact that some children in the class were more intellectual and academically advanced than others, the teachers would generally permit students to work at their own pace whenever possible.

When lunchtime came, Sebastian and Adam sat downstairs in the spacious dining hall with their classmates. Sebastian lifted up his shirt to show them the scar from his appendix operation.

"Ugh, gross!" they laughed.

"Hello chaps!" David said, joining them at the table. "Mr Stevens asked me to distribute these," he continued and started handing out some sheets of paper. As he munched on a banana, Sebastian picked up one of the sheets and read through it. 'International Essay Writing Competition!' it said at the top of the page. It stated that the competition was open to children under 14 years of age and that entrants could write an essay on any topic they wished. The word limit was 1,500 words and the winner would receive a prize of £200. "If any of you do decide to enter, leave the completed essay with the school secretary and she will post it to the judges," David said.

His interest piqued, Sebastian was about to ask his fellow students if anyone could think of a good topic to write about, but David cut across him. "My parents and I are going to our country house this evening for a game of polo. Any of you fancy coming along to watch?"

All the children at the table began pleading with him to be allowed go. "Oh yes! I love polo!" Adam said excitedly. But Sebastian said that he'd give it a miss, as he wanted to start work on the essay. He carefully folded the piece of paper and placed it in his blazer pocket.

Becoming bored with the current conversation, Sebastian began telling everyone about a programme he had recently watched on television about astronomy, and commented that he would like to be a scientist when he grew up.

"Are scientists paid well?" David asked.

"I don't really know," Sebastian replied, never having actually thought about it before.

All the children began asking each other what they wanted to work at when they grew up and about how much money they were likely to make working in the respective professions.

"I want to be a solicitor," Sayeeda said.

"I think I'd like to work in a bank – because I'm good at maths," Theresa, a pale girl with medium-length brown hair, commented.

"I want to be the Minister for Education!" Michael avowed with a smirk.

Everyone burst into giggles at the absurdity of this notion. Sebastian began to zone out and started thinking about the essay competition and what he'd write about. When the students returned to their classroom, it was time for a French lesson.

"*Bonjour les enfants*," Mrs Hamilton, the French teacher said as she entered to room.

"*Bonjour Madame*," everyone replied. The teacher tried to start the lesson, but noticed that Michael was chatting to fellow student George, who was sitting beside him.

"Michael!" Mrs Hamilton snapped.

"Sorry," Michael murmured, and then went quiet. He managed to behave himself for the remainder of the school day, which consisted of a still-life art lesson with Mr Rogers and a computer class with Mr Tilford.

Later that day, when Sebastian arrived home from school, he told his parents about the essay writing competition and they both agreed that he should enter it. When he informed them that he was stuck for a topic to write about, Mr Howard suggested writing a paper about how to run a successful business. Sebastian found the topic a bit too dull, but thanked his father for the suggestion anyway. Mrs

Howard looked over at him from the kitchen sink where she was filling a vase of flowers with water. "Maybe have a look through the books in the living room; you might get some ideas there," she said with a smile.

Sebastian scanned his eyes along the dozens of books in the mahogany bookcase. The majority of them were his father's and covered topics such as entrepreneurial skills, politics, getting the most out of employees, etc. Eventually, a book caught his eye. It was a leather-bound history book about the abolition of the slave trade. He slowly pulled it out from its resting place and began to turn over its gold-gilded pages. After reading the first chapter, he sat down at the computer, opened the word processor and typed an opening paragraph of his essay. He worked throughout the afternoon, reading up on the slave trade and making notes. When bedtime arrived, Sebastian got cosy under his sheets and eagerly awaited the sound of his parents' footsteps on the staircase. The pair came into his room, dimmed the lights, and sat down together at the end of his bed. Mrs Howard picked up the book of folktales from her son's bedside cabinet and she and her husband took turns reading him *Little Red Riding Hood*.

* * *

On Thursday morning, Sebastian woke early. Although it was a typical school day, it was also a very special day – 23rd April. When he arrived into class all his classmates began wishing him a happy birthday.

"It's your birthday?" Michael asked, looking surprised.

This proved to be an awkward moment for Sebastian, for with the exception of Michael, he had invited all the children in his class to attend his birthday party later that afternoon. Of course he had contemplated inviting him, but eventually decided against it because he was so mischievous.

"Remind me what time your party starts?" David asked, rushing over to Sebastian. Sebastian coughed loudly.

"So, how are your parents these days?" he responded, briefly flicking his eyes towards Michael.

"They're fine, why?" David asked, thinking it an odd question given that Sebastian had never actually met his parents.

Seconds later, Mr Stevens arrived and everyone took their places. The headmaster told the class to take out their copy of *Fairy Tales*. He asked Theresa to read aloud a story called *The Little Match Girl*. Theresa turned to the relevant page and was about to begin when the sound of flatulence erupted from the back of the room. All the children burst into a chorus of muffled sniggers.

"That does it!" Mr Stevens shrieked angrily. Without even asking who was responsible, he bounded towards Michael, who was fumbling desperately to put something into his schoolbag. The teacher grabbed the offending item from him and held it up in for all the class to see. It was a red whoopee cushion. "I want you to stay behind after school today, Michael. I will be contacting your parents about your antics," he said, picking up Michael's ruler and tapping it lightly against his desk.

Michael gulped.

During lunch, Sebastian and one of his classmates, Maria, played a game of chess while they ate, and then it was time for music lessons. The class gathered in the music room and picked up their respective instruments, which included: violins, cellos, flutes, clarinets, and trumpets. The music teacher was a wispy-haired old man called Mr Godfrey. Sebastian took his place at the piano and began to tinkle away. Soon the room was filled with the sound of music as the children warmed up. Iain, one of the violin players, broke a string and so everybody waited patiently until he replaced it. During the lesson proper, the class played simple renditions of classical pieces by Beethoven, Chopin, and Holst. All the while, Mr Godfrey kept a steady beat on percussion.

After the music lesson, the students sat through a few more classes, including a geography class (with Mrs Evans) about different types of rocks and minerals, and a maths class with Mr Nuttall that focused on fractions. When school finished for the day, the students began making their way down the school's staircase and spilling into the entrance hall where Mr Stevens was taking to Michael and his parents. A group of children were lingering nearby, trying to hear what Michael's parents and the headmaster were saying. Sebastian joined them and turned his ear towards the adults.

"We're terribly sorry that Michael is causing trouble. We will fully support any punishment you feel is appropriate,"

Michael's mother said to Mr Stevens. Becoming aware of the boys and girls staring over, the headmaster began gesturing towards the door, prompting the students to continue on their way.

Throughout the afternoon, the Howards' front doorbell rang continuously as more and more children arrived. All Sebastian's friends sang *Happy Birthday*, and after he had blown out all 10 candles on his birthday cake, it was time to open his presents. He excitedly opened each one in turn, unwrapping toys, board games, and books. David had bought him a glossy poster of the solar system, while Adam had bought him a book of puzzles called *The Big Book of Puzzles: Critical Thinking Extravaganza!*

However, there was still one more present left; the gift from his parents.

"Happy Birthday Sebastian!" his parents exclaimed, handing it to him. Sebastian quickly ripped off the blue wrapping paper to reveal a box with the image of a microscope on the front.

"Oh wow! Thank you so much!" he cried in delight. He opened the wooden box and took out the various components of the microscope. He immediately assembled the apparatus and began to look at the numerous slides of plant and insect specimens.

Throughout the afternoon, the children played charades, musical chairs and board games, and stuffed themselves with cake, toffees, jellies, and gingerbread men. While the children were trying to decide what game to play next,

Mr Howard asked Adam about his father's new racehorse. Adam had just started to tell him about Hayek when Mrs Howard pointed out that it was a glorious day outside, and suggested that the children should all go the park and take advantage of the sunshine.

The children agreed that an adventure in the park was a good idea. Mrs Howard gave them a bag of bread so that they could feed the ducks, and then off they went. They walked the short distance to the local park and passed through the arched entrance. The park was bustling, with a festival in full swing. The air smelled of candyfloss and popcorn, families picnicked and children ran about flying kites in the sky. Blackbirds and robins hopped from tree to tree, gathering twigs for their nests, and a brass band marched along the footpath by the park's algae-infested pond. The musicians, wearing red tunics, white belts and tall black furry hats, played their instruments as they marched.

There was an array of stalls selling refreshments and children's toys. Sebastian bought a plastic toy sword and Adam bought a stuffed, red dragon. The rest of the children gathered around in a circle as the two boys rolled about on the grass, fighting a make-believe fantasy battle. Adam held the dragon firmly in his hand and kept lunging it towards Sebastian, who battled to keep the beast at bay with his sword. Eventually he grabbed the dragon, threw it to the ground and jabbed the sword into it. Everybody cheered.

When they got bored of the game, the children fed little pieces of bread to the ducks in the pond and then sat on the grass chatting and watching the world go by. By early evening, things began to wind down in the park, and so the children made their way back to Sebastian's house. They spent half an hour playing hide and seek, but then the doorbell started ringing as the children's parents arrived to collect them.

Sebastian shook hands with each of his friends as they left, and thanked them again for their gifts. Eventually only Adam was left. Sebastian picked up the puzzle book that he had bought him and began to look through all the riddles, brainteasers and odd-one-out puzzles. He stopped on a random page and Adam and his parents gathered behind him, peering over his shoulder. There were five pictures: a square, a triangle, a circle, a rectangle and a star. Beneath them was a sentence, which read 'Which is the odd one out?' Sebastian rested his chin on his hand and began to think.

Mr Howard leant down close to his son. "Carefully discriminate between the shapes, Sebastian. Remember, the ability to discriminate is the bedrock of critical thinking," he said.

"I think the odd one out..." Sebastian began, and then hesitated for a second. "I think the odd one out is the circle, because it's the only one that doesn't have straight edges." He looked up the answers at the back of the book and confirmed that the circle was indeed the correct answer.

"Well done Sebastian!" everyone said.

But soon it was time for Adam to go home. It was getting late and he was feeling tired.

Sebastian again expressed his gratitude for the book of puzzles as his friend left.

"Glad you like it" Adam replied.

As his parents tucked him into bed that night, Sebastian told them that he had had a wonderful birthday and thanked them for the microscope. Although he was exhausted, he pleaded with them to read him a bedtime story before he went to sleep.

"Absolutely not!" Mr Howard declared. "You're 10 now – definitely too old for that sort of thing."

"But it's my birthday..." Sebastian said solemnly, trying to look as sad as possible.

Mrs Howard took a hold of her husband by the sleeve of his shirt and pulled him over towards the bed, "Your father and I aren't so mean that we wouldn't read you a bedtime story on your birthday," she said. And so, the couple sat down and read him *Rumpelstiltskin.*

CHAPTER 2

One weekday evening in late May, as Sebastian was studying a leaf under his microscope, his parents came into the room looking exceptionally spruced-up. Mrs Howard told him to put on his suit, but she wouldn't say why. Feeling excited, Sebastian ran up to his bedroom and rummaged around in his wardrobe until he found the outfit. He quickly changed into it and when he arrived back downstairs, the Smith family were in the hallway chatting to his parents.

The adults told their sons that they had a surprise for them; a night at the opera. Sebastian was elated and threw his arms up in excitement. Although the Smiths were regular operagoers, Sebastian had never been, although he and his parents often went to the theatre. Adam was excited too, not so much at the thought of watching another opera, but mainly to have another child come along with him this time.

The families made their way out into the driveway and waited as Mr Howard locked the front door. A pair of policemen on their beat passed by the house, "Hope you have a good night," one of the officers said, noticing how well-dressed the family members were.

"Thank you," everyone replied.

The two families piled into Mrs Howard's Range Rover and set off for the city centre, with Mrs Howard at the wheel. They traversed past parks, children's playgrounds and shopping centres, and under railway bridges. The roads became busier as they advanced towards the heart of the city.

The car crawled along at a snail's pace in the heavy traffic. Mr Smith chatted to Mr and Mrs Howard about a business trip he would shortly taking to New York City (Mr Smith's parents were from New York and he usually flew back and forth to the city once or twice a year). Sebastian and Adam stared out the windows, taking in the sights of the bustling city streets. Hordes of pedestrians rushed about while others idly window-shopped, and newspaper sellers plied their trade on almost every corner. Only murals of the new government regime's party logo (a red rose) painted onto walls hinted at the political strife bubbling beneath the veneer of everyday life.

At one point, they passed a new building that was still under construction. The structure was colossal. Three watchtowers rose up into the sky and a barbed-wire fence was beginning to take shape around the building's perimeter. Men and women clad in harnesses and other safety equipment were busy at work. Some operated heavy-duty machinery, while others pushed wheelbarrows full of bricks and tools. Showers of sparks reigned down from some scaffolding and the deafening rumble of drilling reverberated through the air.

Feeling curious, Sebastian reached out to his father sitting in the front passenger seat and tugged on his jacket. "Daddy, what's that building?" he asked loudly so as to be heard over the drilling. Mr Howard put on his spectacles and looked out through the window.

"Oh yes, I read about it in the newspaper," he said. "It's the new rehabilitation centre. It's a bit like a prison, but as its name suggests, it focuses on rehabilitating criminals rather than punishing them."

Sebastian shuddered as he thought about all the violent and dangerous criminals that the centre would hold when it was completed.

Eventually, they arrived in the vicinity of the opera house, but had difficulty finding a parking space. So they parked a few streets away and continued on foot through the city's winding thoroughfares, the adults holding their children's hands whenever they crossed roads. Sebastian and Adam kept stopping to look in through the windows of cafes and sweet shops they encountered, which compelled their parents to turn around and call after them several times. By now the sun was beginning to set, producing a red tinge in the evening sky.

Finally, they arrived at the magnificent opera house. An attendant opened the door for them and gave a polite smile as they walked on through. Mrs Howard handed the tickets to an usher who led them upstairs to the balcony area and showed them to their seats.

The opera house was packed. Sebastian was in awe at the grandeur of his surroundings, with red seat coverings and gold-leaf plasterwork all around. He cast his eyes upwards at a huge glass dome on the ceiling, out through which he could see the darkening skies above. Sebastian then looked down over the balcony at the rows and rows of people sitting below. Like he and his companions, they were all immaculately groomed and dressed in suits, tuxedos, and flowing dresses. The air was filled with the sound of chatting, but then the lights started to dim and a hush descended. A voice, transmitted through the speaker-system, anounced that the performance was about to commence and asked everyone to switch off their mobile phones. Then the enormous red curtains opened, revealing a cast of performers dressed in elaborate costumes. They began to act out various roles, taking turns singing in Italian to an orchestral accompaniment.

Sebastian was fascinated by the props and background scenery, and listened carefully to the lyrics, trying to follow the storyline. Mrs Smith was moved to tears by the emotive performance, and Sebastian took a handkerchief from his pocket and handed it to her. During the interval, the Howards and Smiths went to the bar where the adults (except Mrs Howard, who was driving) enjoyed glasses of champagne and sparkling wine. Adam and Sebastian both had an orange juice. They chatted as they drank and the two boys agreed that they were enjoying the performance thus far. Adam, more knowledgeable of operas than Sebastian, explained the intricacies of operatic enactments to him and filled him in on the parts of the storyline that he'd missed.

After about half an hour, everyone returned to their seats and watched the remainder of the performance. As Sebastian understood it, the opera was about a young maiden with whom two men were in love; a rich but immoral prince, and a kind-hearted poor man. She has to choose between the two, and in the end chose the poorer man. Although

Sebastian generally enjoyed watching the performance, he got a bit bored on several occasions. At the opera's finale, everyone in the audience stood up and clapped. Before they left, the Howards and Smiths mingled for a few minutes, making chit-chat with some of the other operagoers. The adults asked Sebastian what he had thought of the opera.

"It was very good, but I felt it could have been a bit shorter," he replied.

The adults all laughed.

By the time the two families exited the opera house, it was almost 11 o'clock. Although the sky was pitch-black, the streets were illuminated by the glow of streetlamps. Other than the crowds leaving the opera house, the city was relatively deserted. The two families started making their way back to where Mrs Howard's Range Rover was parked, with the two boys leading the way. Everyone was tired, and the only sounds were those of their footsteps and occasional dripping from nearby gutters.

As they were approaching Mrs Howard's car, Sebastian became aware of a dark shape sprawled across the ground. He initially assumed that it was a black rubbish bag that had been knocked over, but as he got closer he realised that it was a person.

"Look!" he shouted, pointing ahead. Everybody stopped in their tracks and peered through the darkness trying to get a better look at who, or what, was lying on the ground.

"Wait here while we take a look," Mr Howard said, beckoning to Mr Smith.

The boys and their mothers stood a short distance back, while the two men went to investigate. They leant down and began to gently nudge the person with their hands. When it was clear that there was no danger, the rest of the group crept forward.

In the dim light, Sebastian could see that it was a dishevelled man on the ground. He looked like a tramp, with tattered clothes and a stubbly chin. Resting beside him was an empty gin bottle.

"Oh the poor soul" Mrs Howard said.

The tramp's arm twitched slightly and everyone breathed a sigh of relieve that he was alive.

"Is he alright?" Adam's mother asked.

"Yes. Although I think he's had too much to drink," her husband replied. "But he'll be fine. I know a place where we can take him." Mr Howard and Mr Smith gently lifted the man to his feet. He started to sway from side to side and began mumbling incoherently, but the two men kept him propped up.

The two families and the tramp made their way down the street, passing row after row of old, pebble-dashed buildings. The boys' fathers helped to keep the tramp steady as he walked. After a few dozen yards, they stopped outside one of the buildings. 'Hostel for the Homeless' read a sign above the door. The two men helped the unsteady man up the large granite steps and towards the doorway, which was flanked by two marble pillars. The man wobbled with each step, and Sebastian and Adam lent a hand to keep him balanced. The main door of the building was open, and in the hallway was an old woman sitting and working at a desk.

She looked up and rushed towards the doorway. "I think this man needs a bed for the night, and may also need some medical attention," Sebastian's father told her.

"Don't worry, we'll take good care of him here," the old woman said with a smile. With that, she threw a blanket over the tramp's shoulders and began to lead him inside.

Suddenly, the man stopped and turned around. He put his hand on one of the marble pillars to steady himself. "God bless you all," he said in a slurred tone, and then disappeared in through the doorway.

As the Howards and Smiths walked briskly along the lonely streets, back to Mrs Howard's car, Sebastian asked Mr Smith how he knew about the hostel.

"Your father and I are patrons of that organisation," he replied. "We give them money every year. They wouldn't survive without donations."

When the two families arrived back at the car, they climbed in, and Sebastian again sat in the back with the Smiths. As everyone was feeling quite tired, there wasn't much chat between them as they cruised along the quiet streets. Sebastian rested his chin on his hands and stared dozily out the window, watching the city lights flicker by. He could hear a low rumbling sound that seemed to be getting louder and louder. Curious, he leaned right up against the glass.

Up ahead was an area of the city that was particularly brightly lit. As they grew closer, he realised that it was the new rehabilitation centre. Construction work continued under the brightness of huge spotlights and the sound of drilling echoed through the air. Sebastian looked at his watch.

"Isn't it strange that they're still working at this time?" he asked to no one in particular as he turned back around.

"Uh-huh," his mother affirmed from the driver's seat.

"I guess…" Adam replied with a yawn.

Of the three other adults, only Mr Smith was alert enough to respond. He looked at Sebastian and nodded. "Yes, it's unusual," he said sleepily, and then closed his eyes and lay his head down on his wife's shoulder.

In due course, they arrived home and Mrs Howard parked in the driveway. The two families bid each other goodnight and the Smiths headed back to their own house.

The Howards felt tired, and began getting ready for bed. As Sebastian hung his suit up in the wardrobe, he kept thinking about poor old tramp, and imagining what it would be like to have no home. His parents tucked him in and kissed him goodnight, and gently closed the bedroom door as they left. As they no longer indulged him by reading him bedtime stories, after they had left, Sebastian picked up his book of folk tales, took out the bookmark and read himself *Cinderella*.

* * *

The next morning at breakfast, Sebastian noticed that his parents were unusually quiet. However, he didn't think much of it, assuming that they were still tired from the night at the opera.

Whilst Sebastian finished his toast, which was spread with a generous portion of his favourite sticky jam, his father rose from the table and said, "I need to leave now. I have to attend an important meeting at the asphalt plant."

Sebastian was about to ask what the meeting was about, but when he looked up from his breakfast his father was gone. Through the open kitchen window, Sebastian could hear the sound of footsteps on the driveway and then a car door slam shut.

"Do you know what his meeting is all about?" he asked his mother, who was sweeping the kitchen floor. But Mrs Howard was lost in her thoughts and didn't reply.

At school that morning, Mr Carson taught a history lesson focusing on the Second World War. He adhered a map of the world to the blackboard and pointed out the Allied and Axis powers. He explained to the class how the Allies had defeated the Nazis and liberated the countries they had occupied.

William, a pug-nosed boy with a bob of fair hair, raised his hand. "Wasn't there an event afterwards called the Cold War, sir?" he asked.

"That's correct," Mr Carson replied. "It was the hostility between Soviet Russia and the West." The teacher pointed out on the map the various countries in each of the Communist and Western blocs.

"The failure of socialism in the Soviet Union proved once and for all the superiority of the capitalist system," he stated categorically. All the children in the class nodded. The teacher spent a few more minutes denouncing socialism and praising the virtues of the capitalist mode of production, and then asked if there were any questions. But so convincing was his rhetoric that there were none.

Hence, the children moved onto a science class that was followed by a geography lesson, and then mathematics. Before school ended for the day, the class read some more of Hans Christian Anderson's fairy tales with Mr Stevens, discussing and debating the moral of each story until the school bell sounded.

When Sebastian arrived home, his father was in the kitchen talking to someone on the telephone and his mother was sifting through a pile of papers on the kitchen table. As it seemed that they weren't free to talk, Sebastian sat down at the computer in the living room and continued writing his essay for the competition. As he typed, he could overhear his father speaking, and the tone of his voice told him that something was wrong. Sebastian crept out into the hallway and closed his eyes to heighten his sense of hearing.

"... you would think that with all the jobs we've created over the years they'd want the plant to stay operational. But all they've done is strangle us with red tape..." Sebastian now knew for certain that something was seriously wrong. His father continued, "So many rules and regulations, so much over-the-top health and safety nonsense, so much mindless bureaucracy. They've ruined everything!" Sebastian walked into the kitchen but his mother quickly shooed him back out and shut the door. He stood in the hall, listening intently, trying to make out what his father's muffled voice was saying. When his father had finished the phone call, Sebastian slowly opened the kitchen door.

"Alright, you can come in now," his father said.

"I was talking to our solicitor," he said, sitting solemnly at the kitchen table. Sebastian nodded. "Our asphalt plant has gone into liquidation," Mr Howard continued and held his hand up to his forehead. "The new government has been making things *very* difficult for businesses. A few weeks ago, health and safety officials started nit-picking every single safety procedure at the plant. Your mother and I didn't tell you before now because we didn't want you to worry."

Sebastian felt a cold chill run through his entire body.

"How are we going to make money?" was the first question he thought to ask.

"Don't worry, there's no need to panic," Mr Howard said. "We have enough savings to keep us to going for a while, until I find a job."

The couple spent most of the remainder of the afternoon looking through the accounts relating to the plant and making phone calls. Later that evening the Smiths called round to offer the family their condolences on the closure of the business. "If you need anything, anything at all, you need just ask," Mrs Smith said. "Isn't that right?" she added, looking at her husband.

"Yes, of course" he replied, "but to tell you the truth, we're not doing too well ourselves at the moment. Some of the businesses we own are beginning to falter under the weight of all the new government regulation." Mrs Smith put her hand on her husband's and caressed it gently. When the Smiths had left, Mrs Howard told Sebastian that he might as well continue writing his essay, as sitting around worrying wouldn't achieve anything.

* * *

The next few days at school were tough as the closure of the asphalt plant played on Sebastian's mind. Adam cracked jokes in an attempt to cheer him up, but to little avail. It was only a few weeks till the end of the school year, and so Sebastian decided to buckle down. Each evening he would sit at his bedroom desk, complete his homework, and then study for the summer exams. In his free time he would do some work on his essay for the competition. He borrowed a few books about the slave trade from the local library and carefully cross-checked each piece of information (such as the year the Act of Parliament which abolished the trade was passed, etc.) to ensure that it was correct before incorporating it into the essay.

* * *

When the time came for Mr Howard to pay one final visit to the plant, Sebastian pleaded to be allowed accompany him.

When they arrived, his father handed him a hard hat and told him to put it on. Things were very quiet at the plant and the handful of workers who were present were packing crates and boxes into the back of trucks and dismantling pieces of machinery. Four of them came over to Mr Howard and gave him a bottle of wine wrapped with a ribbon.

"You shouldn't have," he told them, "especially under the circumstances".

The men each shook hands with their former boss and thanked him for all he had done for them over the years. They told him that they were very unlikely to find new jobs, but asked if he would give them references if they needed them.

"Of course," Mr Howard replied. "Anything I can do to help."

* * *

The next big event on the school calendar was sports day. It was exceptionally hot that day and the smell of freshly-cut grass hung in the air around the school grounds. Parents were busy lathering coats of sunscreen onto their children's faces and arms, and the teachers went about organising children into groups. Soon children were sprinting along the white-painted racetracks and jumping over hurdles. A boy called Jeremy, who had recently taken a course in first aid, went around attending to scratches and bruises.

Sebastian and some classmates were sheltering from the sun under a sycamore tree as they waited for their competitions to begin.

"Hey, look everyone! Michael is doing an impression of a tomato!" Adam shouted.

They all turned around and looked at Michael who stood a few feet away, leaning against railings at the edge of the sports field, his face bright red with sunburn.

"No flies on you Adam…" Michael quipped.

"Well, there certainly won't be any on you Michael. Not with that sunburn anyway. They'd most likely disappear in a puff of smoke!" Adam replied. Everyone burst into laughter. Even Michael couldn't prevent a little smile appearing onto his face.

"You crack me up Adam," he chuckled.

Michael joined the other children under the shade of the tree and Sebastian asked him which events he would be participating in.

"Mr Stevens told me I'm not allowed to take part," he replied in a huff. "It's my punishment for all the pranks I pulled this year." As the children bantered, Eric came plodding over. He was sweating profusely and breathless from the sack race he had just participated in.

"Apparently this school is going to close soon," he said out of the blue as he stuffed a cheese and pickle sandwich into his mouth.

Everyone fell silent.

"What!?" William asked. "Who told you that?"

"I overheard those children over there say it earlier," Eric replied, pointing to some children in the distance who were chatting with the school's gardener.

Puzzled, the students began asking each other if anyone else had heard the rumour, but no one had.

"It sounds a bit ridiculous," David said, looking towards Eric. "Why on earth would the school close? And anyway, if it was going to close for some reason, our teachers would have told us."

Just then, Mr Stevens began calling out the names of the children who would be participating in the next event, which was the egg and spoon race. Sebastian and Adam were called and so went with some fellow students to the start line and delicately balanced eggs on their spoons. When Mr Stevens blew his whistle, they all began to run. Most of them found themselves having to stop frequently to pick up their eggs after they dropped to the ground. One student called Christopher had only taken a few steps when he dropped his egg and then accidently stood on it, smashing the shell. Sebastian made it about halfway towards the finish line before he dropped his, while Adam made it a few feet further. In the end it was David who won the race and received a trophy of a gold hand holding an egg and spoon.

The next competition was the three-legged race, and Sebastian and Adam ended up paired together. The boys' parents cheered them on from the side-lines, but unfortunately they didn't fare any better in that event either, coming second last after Sayeeda and Eric. Sebastian and Adam competed in a few other sporting events, but by the end they had won nothing. They both felt a bit disappointed but made sure to congratulate David for his victory in the egg and spoon race.

The last event to be held was the teachers' race. All the teachers at the school, except Mr Whittaker, Mr Rogers and Mr Tilford (who said they were too old to run), took their places behind the white line, and when a parent, who was acting as referee, blew a whistle, they sprinted forward. Mr Stevens took an early lead, and his black gown fluttered behind him as he ran. Music teacher Mr Godfrey couldn't keep up with his colleagues and ended up trailing behind, while Mr Carson stumbled and crashed to the ground. Mrs Evans made it about halfway along the track before she developed a stitch in her side and had to stop. For a time Mr Stevens, Mrs Hamilton and Mr Nuttall were all neck and neck, but it was the school's headmaster who crossed the finish line first. Everyone applauded as Mr Stevens was handed his award cup and held it proudly up in the air.

"Hard luck Sebastian, maybe next year," his parents said as the trio walked back to their house. As they walked, Sebastian's father brought the conversation around to the upcoming examinations, pointing out that these were much more important than winning prizes at sports day.

The family stopped briefly at a local newsagent so Mr Howard could buy a newspaper, and then continued on home. Sebastian immediately sat down at the computer in the living room and went about putting the finishing touches on his essay. Within a few minutes it was all done. He felt a sense of satisfaction come over him, but just as he was printing off a copy his mother and father rushed into the room, his father holding the newspaper.

"Quickly! Turn on the television!" Mr Howard said in a fluster.

"What wrong!?" Sebastian asked, momentarily overcome by a slight panic. Such was the look of horror on his parents' faces that for a split-second he genuinely thought maybe the world was about to end.

"The government is going to abolish private education!" his mother explained, her voice quivering.

"Oh?" Sebastian responded as he breathed a sigh of relief. Mr Howard picked up the remote control and turned on the television. On virtually every station, reporters were discussing this news. They said that all private education was to be abolished, although emphasised that things would continue as normal until the end of the current school year.

"First the asphalt plant and now this!" Mr Howard said through gritted teeth.

"So my school is going to close?" Sebastian asked as the gravity of the new government policy began to sink in.

"Yes!" his father responded in an uncharacteristically angry tone.

"That's so unfair!" Sebastian declared. "I'll miss all my friends and teachers, especially Mr Stevens." As Sebastian continued to whinge, Mr Howard began to pace back and forth across the living room floor.

"I need to go for a walk to clear my head," he said and promptly left the house.

Sebastian turned to his mother and was about to start moaning to her, but when he noticed the anguish in her eyes he decided to say nothing. Instead, he picked up the printed pages of his essay that had by now been fully printed and punched a staple through the top left hand corner. He then folded it in half and put it in his schoolbag.

When Mr Howard returned from his walk, he told Sebastian to tidy his bedroom because it was starting to look like a pigsty. Realising that his father was in a bad mood, Sebastian didn't object and immediately did as he was asked.

* * *

The next day, school was abuzz with everyone talking about the fact that private education was to be abolished. Mr Stevens looked glum as he stood at the front of the class. "I expect you've all heard by now that this school is to close," he said.

Everyone nodded or otherwise confirmed that they had heard the news.

"There will be an emergency meeting held here in the school this evening. Please tell your parents that I would appreciate their attendance."

Mr Stevens began the day's lessons, and when lunchtime came, Sebastian made his way to the secretary's office and handed in his entry for the international essay writing competition. The secretary, Mrs Wheeler, was a frail old woman who liked to natter with anybody who strayed within her vicinity. "Isn't it terrible what the government has done?" she asked as she handed Sebastian a form to complete.

"Yes, it is, Mrs Wheeler…" Sebastian replied. "My parents were very put out by the news." Sebastian continued chatting to the secretary as he wrote his name, date of birth and home address on the relevant sections of the entry form. When he was done he handed the page back to Mrs Wheeler who assured him that his essay would be received by the judges before the competition's deadline (which was still a few weeks away).

That evening, Mr and Mrs Howard and Adam's parents attended the emergency meeting at the school. Sebastian spent the time round at the Smiths' residence, where Adam's grandmother minded the two boys. Sebastian and Adam spent the evening studying, but did manage to take time out to enjoy some cookies Mrs Smith had left out for them. Eventually, the Howards and Smiths returned from the meeting. They said that the main purpose of the event had been to help parents organise new schools for their children.

Sebastian and Adam's parents were given the details of their new assigned school, which was in the heart of the city, and both boys were now enrolled. Or more precisely, they were provisionally enrolled as there was still some paperwork that their parents needed to complete, but that was just a formality. The Howards and Smiths found out that David had also been assigned a place in the same school.

"At least there will be another friendly face there," Adam said to Sebastian.

* * *

The next week of school passed uneventfully and then it was exam time. All the students were somewhat anxious on the morning of the first examination, and dozens sat in their classrooms and in the dining hall doing some last minute cramming. When the time came, everyone made their way to the examination hall and sat down at a desk. An invigilator went around handing out the exam papers and everyone got to work answering the various questions. By the end of the week, Sebastian was satisfied that he had done reasonably well in each of his exams.

* * *

On the last day of school there were no classes. Mr Stevens had decided to throw a reception for the students, parents and teachers. There was a celebratory mood of sorts at the event with balloons and finger-food everywhere – the headmaster said he wanted private education to go out with a bang rather than a whimper. Students and their parents shook hands with the school staff and expressed their gratitude for all their hard work throughout the years. The Howards got chatting to Mr Stevens, and Sebastian told him that he had entered the international essay writing competition.

"That's great," the headmaster replied. "What's the essay about?"

Sebastian informed him that it was about the abolition of the slave trade, and went on to explain how he had researched the topic and used different sources to cross-check all the important historical details. Mr Stevens commended Sebastian on seeing the essay through to completion and wished him the best of luck in the competition.

Shortly before the gathering concluded, Mr Stevens stood up at the front of the large reception hall and wished all the children the best for the future. However, he warned them that life at their new schools would probably be quite different than what they were accustomed to. Just as everyone was getting ready to leave, Michael rushed up to the headmaster with a serious look on his face and tugged at his cape. "I want to tell you that I'm sorry for being such a troublesome student," he said. "I'm going behave myself from now on."

"I'm glad to hear that young man," Mr Stevens replied, giving Michael a firm pat on the shoulder.

* * *

Even with the closure of the family's business and the abolition of private education, life continued as normal for Sebastian through the summer as the family lived off their savings. His parents took him for visits to museums and art galleries. They also took several trips out of the city, mostly to seaside resorts where they went paddling in the sea and built castles in the sand. Sebastian especially liked to look for crabs and little fish lurking at the bottom of rock pools. Sebastian also met up with Adam and David regularly during the summer. The boys' parents encouraged this given that they would all be starting the same school after the holidays. The boys played games of Scrabble and mucked about in Adam's tree house.

Despite Sebastian's seemingly carefree existence, the economy was going into severe recession and many adults were out of work, including his father. Mr Howard told his wife and son that he was holding out for a job appropriate for someone of his intellectual ability and management experience.

Sebastian's exam report card arrived in the post one sunny morning. He had received mainly As and Bs, but also two Cs. It was a reasonably good result, but as his parents pointed out, there was room for improvement. As the summer holidays drew to an end and the new school year got closer, Sebastian spent more time thinking about Mr Stevens and how he would miss his old school. Eventually, 'Back to School' displays began appearing in shop windows throughout the city, providing Sebastian, Adam and David with a constant reminder of the inevitable.

CHAPTER 3

A few days before the school year proper began, Sebastian and his mother attended an induction day at the new school. Sebastian knew he would see Adam and Mrs Smith there, but David and his parents had other commitments so were unable to attend. Mrs Howard drove with her son in her Range Rover through the city's early morning traffic until they finally reached their destination. They found a space in the busy car park and then walked together towards the ugly grey school building. As they approached, Sebastian noticed graffiti dotted about the walls. "*This doesn't look very promising...*" he thought.

The pair walked into the reception area and were immediately greeted by a grinning man who introduced himself as Mr Wallace, the school's head teacher. Mr Wallace was in early middle age and had short dark hair. He wore a grey suit with a red tie, and spoke with a nasally whine. "And what's your name little man?" he asked condescendingly as he stooped down to Sebastian. When Sebastian replied, Mr Wallace looked up his name on the school's register and confirmed that he was due to begin his final year of junior education at the school, and informed him of his classroom number, which was 6.

Mr Wallace chatted with Sebastian and his mother for a few minutes, and asked Sebastian about his previous schooling. Sebastian explained to his new head teacher that his last school had closed, but that he had studied mathematics, history, Latin, Classics, French, geography, literature, art, computers, music, science, etc. He also mentioned that he had entered an international essay writing competition and was eagerly anticipating the results.

"It all sounds very highbrow!" Mr Wallace said with a laugh.

Sebastian quickly took a dislike to Mr Wallace due to his smug, patronising demeanour, but politely humoured him nevertheless.

New students and their parents continued to flow in, and the head teacher went around introducing himself to one and all. Soon Adam and Mrs Smith showed up, and after Mr Wallace had greeted them and informed Adam of his classroom number (which was the same as Sebastian's and David's), they got chatting to the Howards. When all the attendees had arrived, Mr Wallace stood in front of the group and began by welcoming everyone and reassuring the new students that all the teachers at the school were very nice. But as he was talking, a boy began to pipe up. "I don't want to go to this f#cking school!" he screamed at his mother.

Sebastian and Adam looked around, appalled that anyone, let alone a child, would use such foul language. "I hope that boy won't be in our class," Sebastian whispered to his friend. However, Mr Wallace didn't react to the disturbance and just continued his discourse, which was about the school's ethos.

"The school contains a very diverse student population, but no child is considered better or worse than any other.

Our teachers work strenuously to instil good morals in their students and there is an enormous emphasis placed on building students' self-esteem. For this reason there are no exams - because as everybody knows, poor performance in an examination can permanently diminish a child's sense of self-worth..."

When he asked if there were any questions, Sebastian put up his hand. Mr Wallace looked in his direction and Sebastian asked where he could get his school uniform. But the head teacher informed him that there was no uniform, for uniforms are very old-fashioned and curtail students' personal freedoms too much. So instead, the students were free to wear whatever clothes they liked.

"Can you tell us about the schoolbooks the children will be using? I haven't received any information about them as yet," Mrs Howard said.

"The children will receive their new schoolbooks from their teacher on their first day of term," was Mr Wallace's reply.

Adam's mother then asked, "Will it be necessary for us to pack lunches for our children?"

"No" Mr Wallace told her. "The school has its own canteen and only the food served there is permitted on the school grounds."

After a few more minutes of questions and answers, the induction day concluded. Everybody thanked Mr Wallace as they left, and Sebastian and Adam chatted as they walked with their mothers back to the car park.

"It's not as nice as our old school, is it?" Sebastian asked.

Adam shook his head.

"I don't like Mr Wallace at all..." Sebastian continued.

"Me neither. He's very... very..." Adam replied, searching for an adjective to describe the head teacher.

"Smarmy?" Sebastian suggested.

"Exactly! And he also smells funny!" Adam declared, causing Sebastian to laugh loudly. As they talked, the boy who had made the scene walked past. He continued screaming and swearing at his mother.

"Oh dear..." Mrs Howard said.

Mrs Smith just frowned. They knew that it was impolite to stand there gawking at the commotion, so the foursome got back into their respective cars and set off for home. As they travelled back through the city, Sebastian made it clear to his mother that he wasn't impressed by his new school or by Mr Wallace. She agreed that the head teacher was annoying, but reminded Sebastian that that there was little that could be done since the government had put an end to private education.

* * *

Sebastian spent much of the last weekend of the holidays in Adam's house. In the mornings, the boys painted the walls of the tree house, and in the afternoons they played board games while eating Mrs Smith's home-baked cookies.

On Sunday evening, Sebastian and his parents went for a stroll through the local park. As they walked along the footpath, Mrs Howard gathered up some pieces of litter that were scattered about on the ground and put them in the rubbish bin. Eventually, the sky began to cloud over and drops of rain started to fall, but a beautiful rainbow appeared in the pallid evening sky. As the trio continued along the path they saw a huge parade coming toward them. Scores of people carrying multi-coloured flags and banners were singing and dancing. Mesmerised by all the vibrant colours, Sebastian slowed down as his parents walked on ahead.

When the parade was only a few feet away, one of the men in the procession suddenly lurched forward and grabbed Sebastian. He lifted him up onto his shoulders, causing everyone to clap and cheer. But Sebastian was terrified and began to yell out "Help! Help me!"

Mr and Mrs Howard looked back and saw what was happening. They rushed over and wrestled him off the man's shoulders. "You have no right to manhandle my son like that!" Mr Howard snapped angrily.

"Don't be a party-pooper!" the man replied.

Mrs Howard put her hand on her husband's shoulder and pulled him away. "Rise above it" she whispered.

"Don't mind them," the Howards told their son as they walked back to their house.

* * *

Sebastian woke early on Monday morning, 15 minutes before his alarm went off. He was feeling apprehensive about his first day at his new school but he kept reminding himself that Adam and David would be in his class, which helped quell his anxiety somewhat. He got out of bed and put on a fresh shirt, a V-neck jumper, and pair of brown cord trousers. Downstairs in the hallway, he bumped into his father who was rushing out the door to attend a meeting at the local Jobcentre. Mr Howard wished Sebastian a good first day at school and then left. After eating his breakfast, Sebastian went with his mother out to her car. A fine drizzle was falling as the pair set off to Sebastian's new school. They slowly made their way through the gridlocked early morning traffic, eventually arriving at the school a few minutes before class was due to begin. Mrs Howard stopped in the car park and pulled up the handbrake.

"Hope you enjoy your first day," she said.

With some trepidation, Sebastian opened the passenger door and put his feet down on the tarmac. He headed towards the school building and walked in through the front door. Inside, he found it necessary to force his way through hordes of noisy students milling around in the corridors.

Eventually he found classroom number 6, took a deep breath, and went inside. He was momentarily overwhelmed by the size of the class. There were dozens of students, and their cold, unfriendly eyes stared at him as he made his way towards a desk at the front of the room. Numerous poor-quality crayon drawings adorned the classroom's walls and the air reeked with a foul smell. Sebastian swivelled around in his seat to look again at the other students. They were mostly dressed in tracksuits, hoodie sweatshirts, and in the case of the girls, miniskirts. As he stared, he realised that many of the boys and girls were pointing at him and sniggering. Feeling unnerved, he quickly turned back around.

A few seconds later, David and Adam walked in through the doors and waved over to him. Sebastian breathed a sigh of relief as they sat down at the desks next to him. The boys started to chat, and just as they were expressing their surprise at how many children were in their class, the teacher walked into the room. The boys instinctively went to stand up, but when they realised that everyone else stayed seated, they promptly sat back down again. The teacher was a dour-looking woman with short black hair, pasty skin, and dark circles under her eyes. "I'm Ms Joyce," she said in a monotone as her eyes scanned the room.

Ms Joyce began to sort through some paperwork on her desk. She then turned to Sebastian, mainly because he was the student seated nearest her, and asked him to take a bundle of papers to the school secretary. Sebastian replied that he would happily do so, and asked where he could find her.

"*Her*?" said Ms Joyce sharply. "And what makes you think the school secretary is a woman?" Sebastian said that he had just assumed that the secretary was a woman, as secretaries generally are.

Ms Joyce folded her arms and frowned. "That's just a stereotype," she said. "Stereotyping is one of the lowest forms of bigotry." She informed Sebastian that the school secretary was a *man* called Andy and that *his* office was situated near the school entrance. Sebastian could see that his new teacher was annoyed with him, so he immediately apologised for any offence caused.

Sebastian lifted the bundle of papers from the teacher's desk and made his way down the corridor towards the school's entrance. He located the secretary's office and gave the papers to Andy. Andy was a friendly man, dressed in jeans and a t-shirt, and he had a tattoo on his left bicep.

"Cheers mate!" he said as he took the bundle of paperwork.

Sebastian returned to his classroom and took his seat. In his absence, Adam and David had spoken to Ms Joyce and informed her that they (along with their friend Sebastian) were new students at the school. Adam and David had already introduced themselves to the class, and so Ms Joyce now invited Sebastian to do likewise.

Sebastian stood up and turned to face his peers. "Hello. My name is Sebastian Howard. My old school closed, which is the reason I'm here."

As he spoke, a group of children sitting nearby began making farmyard noises. "Oink! Oink!" one of them squealed. Sebastian looked to Ms Joyce, assuming that she would admonish them, but she said nothing.

"I haven't been in such a big class before, but I look forward to getting to know you all...' he continued. Sebastian and his two friends were shocked by how naughty the other students were.

When Sebastian sat back down, Ms Joyce handed him a stack of schoolbooks. She instructed him to take one and then pass the stack along. The name of the book was *Moral Stories for Kids*. On the front cover was a colourful picture of men, women and children standing in a circle with their hands interlocked. "Please return the books to me at the end of the school day. It's important that they're kept at school," the teacher said.

When all the children had eventually received a copy, Ms Joyce asked the class to turn to the first page. She asked if anybody would volunteer to read the story out loud and Sebastian put his hand up. Ms Joyce did a double-take as she was unaccustomed to children raising their hand in class. But she nodded and Sebastian began to read *Bob the Robber*.

Bob had a hard life. While everybody else spent their time working and buying nice things, Bob just sat in his chair twiddling his thumbs. "Why should everybody else have so much while I have so little?" he thought, feeling sorry for himself. One day Bob was walking down the street when he saw a shiny bicycle chained to some railings. He took a wire-cutter out of his pocket and cut the chain. Suddenly, the bicycle's owner appeared beside him. "There is no need to try and steal my bicycle," the man said. If you really want it so much, I'll give it to you." Tears of happiness ran down Bob's cheeks as he rode off down the street on the bike.

When Sebastian had finished reading, he looked up at Ms Joyce just as a paper airplane whizzed past her head. She didn't react and he assumed that she hadn't noticed it. The teacher pointed to a little blonde-haired girl wearing a baseball cap. "Chantelle, come up to the front of the class and explain the moral of the story Sebastian just read."

Chantelle sighed and muttered as she dragged herself away from her desk and shuffled towards the teacher. Ms Joyce took a little video camera out of her desk drawer and trained it on her. "Now Chantelle, I want you to explain the moral of the story." Chantelle looked into the camera and began to speak. "People become robbers 'cos they have less than everybody else. If people just, you know, shared everything they have with others, no one would have to, like, steal anything – you know what I mean?"

"Oh yes, that was a very good take," said Ms Joyce as she played the recording back on the video camera's little screen.

But Sebastian and his two friends found the moral of the story rather dubious. So Sebastian again raised his hand. "Couldn't an alternative interpretation be that Bob the Robber steals things because he's a very bad, lazy and selfish person?" he asked. All the children in the classroom burst into laughter and a faint smile appeared on Ms Joyce's lips.

"That's such a simplistic explanation," she said. "The reality is much more complicated…" Sebastian tried to question his teacher further regarding the moral lesson, but she just talked over him.

As she was rambling on, a boy began to wail and scream for no apparent reason. Sebastian, Adam and David just stared at him, baffled by his behaviour.

"Shhh Austin," Ms Joyce said softly. But the teacher's soothing words had little effect and Austin started stamping his feet on the floor violently. "Now kids…" Ms Joyce continued, turning back to the rest of the class. "We all know that this country has an excellent health service, but sometimes doctors think they're smarter than everybody else and try to bully people and won't give them their medication. So we will now read a story called *Doctor Daniels*." This time Adam volunteered to read it aloud.

"Show the next patient in," Dr Daniels barked at his secretary.

A woman walked through the surgery door and said, "Excuse me, but I am not your patient, I am your customer." She informed the doctor that she needed a prescription for her pills. However, Dr Daniels said that she didn't need the medication and refused to give her the prescription.

"That's not good enough Tony," the woman replied, calling Dr Daniels by his first name to reinforce the fact that he was no better than anyone else. "If you don't give me the prescription right now, I will make a formal complaint about you."

Dr Daniels quickly wrote out the prescription for his customer, who thanked him as as she paid him his consultation fee.

Ms Joyce called on a boy named Abdul to come up to her desk and explain the moral of the story that he had just heard. Abdul made his way over to Ms Joyce, and when she trained the video camera on him, he began to elucidate the story's moral. Over Austin's wailing, Abdul said, "The doctor's surgery is like a shop – customers come in, ask for what they want and are then given it. But if the doctor doesn't want to give out medicine, customers can threaten the doctor into giving it to them by saying they will complain about them and get them in trouble."

Sebastian, Adam, and David were once more perplexed. Yet again they tried to question Ms Joyce about the story's moral sentiment, and David asked whether the class could discuss the pros and cons of doctors' patients regarding themselves as "customers". However, Ms Joyce wouldn't entertain the idea. Out of curiosity, Adam asked her why she videotaped the children as they explained the morals of the stories. "The video clips are sent to the recently opened rehabilitation centre, where they are used to teach moral values to the inmates," Ms Joyce told him.

The class continued through the morning, reading stories from their schoolbooks. The three boys found the moral of each story baffling, but it was becoming clear to them that Ms Joyce wasn't interested in their opinions. And so they just followed along, feeling increasingly frustrated. At lunchtime, the boys followed all the other children down to the school canteen. The large white canteen contained a long metal counter where meals were served. There were food and drink stains everywhere and, unlike at their old school, the children didn't sit at tables and chat civilly while they ate their lunch; most just wandered around the room shouting and throwing food at each other, while others watched a soap opera on a television attached to the canteen wall.

The three friends stood in the queue and when Sebastian's turn came to order he asked the woman behind the counter if they had roast beef, but she informed him that they didn't. As it turned out that the canteen didn't serve salmon or quail either, Sebastian reluctantly settled for a plate of cod and chips. Adam asked for the same, while David ordered bangers and mash. When the boys had all been served their food, they asked if they had to pay, but the woman informed them that there was no charge. They then took their trays and sat down at a free table, which looked like it hadn't been cleaned for some time.

"Gosh, this school is terrible!" Adam began. "I can't believe how stupid the stories in our books are!"

"I know!" Sebastian replied, "And we're not even allowed debate about them."

"Ms Joyce has virtually no control over the class – no one seems to pay any attention to her," Adam continued as he picked up a knife and fork and cut his portion of fish.

"And what's wrong with that boy, Austin? He acts like a baby," David said.

Adam brushed his fringe away from his eyes and his face formed into a grimace. "Ugh, this food is yucky!" he said in disgust, spitting some fish back down onto his plate.

After managing to eat what they could, the boys put the leftovers in the bin and headed out into the school playground. The playground yard was rectangular in shape and was bordered by high, steel railings. A thick mat of rubber covered the concrete ground. The boys found it difficult to hear each other speak due to the traffic that thundered along the adjacent main road. An elderly gentleman named Mr Redmond supervised yard activities. He wore a beige suit and kept muttering incoherently to himself as he paced back and forth across the playground. Sebastian and his friends suspected that he was a little senile. "No running. You might fall and hurt yourselves," he would say every few seconds. However, most students refused to do as they were told and just ran about anyway. Also a group of children were standing by the railings smoking cigarettes, and no one took any heed.

"That's disgraceful," David whispered to his friends.

Adam nodded and Sebastian tutted.

Shortly after, Mr Redmond began ringing a bell, indicating that lunchtime was over.

When the lessons resumed a few minutes later, Ms Joyce informed the class that they would now be doing sums. (Unlike at their old school, where different teachers taught different subjects, Ms Joyce taught all subjects.)

"Austin struggles a bit with maths. So let's all help him catch up," she said. She took a marker in her hand and began to write simple maths problems on the whiteboard: 5 × 5 = ? Sebastian, Adam, and David immediately put their hands up, but Ms Joyce ignored them and pointed to Austin.

"What is five multiplied by five?" she asked.

Austin didn't reply and just stared vacantly into space. Ms Joyce walked over to his desk and crouched down beside him. She kept prompting him, and said that he should take a guess if he didn't know the answer.

"10?" Austin replied.

Ms Joyce asked him to try again.

This scenario continued for 20 minutes, with Austin unsuccessfully attempting to guess the correct answer. Eventually, Sebastian informed Ms Joyce that his two friends and himself were already well versed in basic multiplication, and politely asked her if they could do more complicated mathematical problems. Immediately, a hiss filled the classroom, and some of the children started to throw paper balls at Sebastian. To his utter shock, Ms Joyce didn't intercede, and simply replied that nobody in the class could move on until Austin had mastered the basics. It wouldn't be fair if he got left behind.

Sebastian was rattled and David and Adam put their hands on his shoulder to comfort him. Austin continued to guess away for a further 15 minutes, until he happened upon the right answer.

"Well done!" Ms Joyce said, and encouraged all the rest of the children in the class to applaud. For a further half an hour, she continued to put simple multiplication problems to Austin, and encouraged him to guess the answers as the other students chatted or played on their mobile phones.

"*I wish we could move on to something more difficult.*" Sebastian thought, and began fidgeting with his pencil.

The class did eventually move on, but only to a simple geography lesson in which Ms Joyce talked about some European countries and their major cities. Ms Joyce had to keep reminding the class of the capitals of most of the countries, as they had forgotten them from previous years' lessons.

"Can anybody remember the capital of Belgium?" she asked the class.

"Stockholm," Chantelle shouted out.

"No, it's Brussels," Ms Joyce informed her, "but you were almost right, well done Chantelle."

By the end of the lesson, nothing had been covered that Sebastian, Adam, or David didn't already know.

At the end of the school day, the teacher set the homework exercise for the class. She picked up a marker and began to write on the whiteboard: "On a sheet of paper, write a short sentence or two saying what you thought of the moral stories we read today." The boys dutifully took note of the homework task in their homework diaries.

Finally, Ms Joyce said that she wanted each student to bring an item of their choosing to school tomorrow for a 'Show and Tell'. They could bring anything they wanted, but nothing sharp or potentially dangerous. By now it was three o'clock, and time for everyone to go home. Before the children left, Ms Joyce took back the *Moral Stories for Kids* schoolbooks and placed them in piles on her desk.

"Well our first day was certainly an experience…" Adam quipped as the boys walked out into the school car park.

"You can say that again!" Sebastian replied.

The three boys looked around the busy car park for a few moments until they saw their mothers' cars.

"See you tomorrow," they said as they parted.

Sebastian hopped into the passenger seat and put on his seatbelt. They set off on their journey home. His mother asked him how his first day at his new school had been.

"I hated it. Everything is so silly and boring!" Sebastian replied in a huff. He proceeded to tell his mother how naughty all the children in his class were, and that the teacher, Ms Joyce, never disciplined them. If a child wanted to go to the toilet they wouldn't bother asking permission, they'd just walk out of the room! And no student was allowed to move beyond simple multiplication arithmetic because one boy was mathematically inept. But worst of all were the ridiculous lessons taught in the schoolbooks!

Mrs Howard acknowledged that it all sounded very odd.

When the pair arrived home, Mr Howard naturally enquired about his son's first day at his new school. Sebastian told him what he had told his mother, and when he told him about the stories in his new schoolbook, Mr Howard agreed that the stories seemed very strange indeed. He was particularly disturbed when Sebastian told him that Ms Joyce filmed students as they explained the morals in the silly stories. But Sebastian's parents advised their son not to make a snap judgement about his new school. He should give it a few weeks, and if things didn't improve, they promised to organise a meeting with his teacher to see if they could resolve the problems.

After dinner, Sebastian went to his room and sat down at his desk. For his homework exercise, he wrote: “I think the stories we read at school today were very silly and set a bad example.” He immediately felt relieved to have gotten his feelings about the stories off his chest and down on paper (even though he knew that Ms Joyce was unlikely to agree). Sebastian spent the rest of the evening solving some of the puzzles in the book that Adam had bought him for his birthday. When eight o’clock came he was feeling dozy. After his parents had said goodnight to him and gone back downstairs, he took his storybook out from the bedside cabinet drawer and read himself *Snow White*.

CHAPTER 4

The next morning, Sebastian marched into school with a positive attitude. He reasoned that if he offered constructive criticisms of the moral stories, Ms Joyce would engage with him. Either way, he had brought his microscope with him for the 'Show and Tell' and looked forward to enlightening his fellow pupils about it. He walked to his classroom and sat down next to Adam and David who had also just arrived. All around them, children were again hollering and shouting.

When Ms Joyce walked in, she started gathering up all the completed homework exercises. Sebastian looked around and took a sneak peek at what some of his classmates had written. Their sentences were riddled with spelling and grammatical errors. However, the consensus seemed to be that the moral stories were "xsellant!" or "brilant!"

"Are you going to grade the exercise?" David asked as Ms Joyce took his homework.

"No, no – your homework is used to help me monitor your progress over the year," she informed him.

Adam rolled his eyes.

When the teacher had collected them all (that is, from the children who had bothered to do their homework), she put the bundle in a box file and then handed out the moral story schoolbooks. The first story they were going to read today was called *Barbara the Babysitter*. She asked

Chantelle to read it out to the class and promised to help her if she got stuck on any big words.

> *For as long as she could remember, it had been Barbara's dream to work with children. When she heard that a local couple were looking for a babysitter for their two sons, she applied for the job and got an interview. But when she finally met the boys' father, she could see that he was annoyed.*
>
> *"According to the background checks I ran, you have been to prison twice!" he said.*
>
> *Barbara felt irate. "You have no right to criticise me for how I behaved in the past," she retorted. "And anyway, I've paid my debt to society. If you don't hire me, I will sue you for discrimination!" The man became very apologetic and immediately offered Barbara the job of babysitter.*

Chantelle read the story slowly, needing much help from Ms Joyce. When she Ms Joyce began to look around the class for someone to explain the story's moral. Sebastian's hand shot straight up, but Ms Joyce ignored him. Instead she asked a little girl called Becky to explain. Becky had long red hair and wore a blue dress with a white collar. She skipped up to the front of the room, and when Ms Joyce pointed her camera at her, she began to speak. "When a person is released from prison, they've paid their debt to society. We have no right to judge someone just because they have been to prison. Ex-convicts should be given the same rights in life as everybody else. If anybody tries to discriminate against them, the criminal should sue them."

Sebastian continued to wave his hand about furiously, trying to attract the teacher's attention. Ms Joyce eventually relented. "Yes Sebastian?" she asked with a sigh.

Sebastian opined that it was inappropriate for someone who had been to prison to babysit children because criminals are, by and large, dangerous and/or irresponsible people.

"Well that's a very offensive thing to say about people who've been to prison," Ms Joyce said, causing all the children to look toward Sebastian and heckle. She then asked if anybody knew how to deal with offensive people.

"Challenge them to a reasoned debate?" David suggested.

"Anybody else?" Ms Joyce asked.

"I know!" Becky shouted out. "Keep a tape recorder hidden in your pocket so you can secretly record everything they say."

"Oh yes, that would be a very clever thing to do" Ms Joyce replied, adding that the tape could then be given to the police. As the class applauded Becky, a boy called Tyrone jumped out of his seat, ran over to Sebastian and started shouting angrily in his face.

"Why is you always so offensive man?!" he kept asking.

Sebastian implored Tyrone to calm down and assured him that he hadn't meant to offend anyone. Ms Joyce told everyone to hush as they were now going to read another story. It was called *Tina the Cranky Teacher*, and this time

Tyrone's twin sister Naomi, a girl with dreadlocked hair and a nose piercing, read it out.

As Tina was teaching her class, a boy called Duncan kept talking and playing with his mobile phone. Tina suddenly let out a roar at poor little Duncan, hurting his feelings. The next morning as the teacher was preparing the day's lessons, Duncan's mother burst into the classroom.

"My perfect little Duncan said that you shouted at him yesterday!" the woman yelled.

Tina trembled nervously. "He was being disruptive and distracting the other students!" she spluttered.

Duncan's mother warned Tina not to raise her voice to her son ever again and then slapped her full force across the face.

"I can't stand bullies!" Duncan's mother shouted as she left the room.

When Naomi was finished, Sebastian apprehensively put his hand up. But alas Ms Joyce just blanked him and asked another child to explain the moral of the story. And so the class continued throughout the morning, reading from the book. Whenever Sebastian, Adam, or David tried to offer a point of view that was different to Ms Joyce's, she would immediately rebuke them. It was becoming clear to the boys that their teacher had no interest in addressing their disquiets about the moral stories.

About halfway through the lesson, there was a knock on the classroom door. Mr Wallace came in and spoke to Ms

Joyce. He said that he had not yet received all her paperwork from yesterday – there were two important forms that were outstanding. The head teacher told her that he needed them immediately and kept clicking his fingers. Ms Joyce hastily sorted through the piles of paper on her desk looking for the relevant forms. As Mr Wallace continued to berate Ms Joyce, Sebastian, David, and Adam looked at each other with eyes opened wide. They were amazed that a school head teacher would treat one of his staff in such as manner, especially in front of her class.

When Mr Wallace finally left, it was time for the 'Show and Tell'. As it turned out, the majority of the children in the class hadn't actually brought anything with them because they hadn't been paying attention to Ms Joyce yesterday. But of those who had bothered to bring something, Ms Joyce reluctantly agreed that Sebastian could start the proceedings. Sebastian carefully took the microscope out of his schoolbag and placed it on his desk. He stood up, turned to face the class, and began to orate about the scientific apparatus. He explained about the different magnification settings, and held up some glass slides containing various materials. As he spoke, he realised that few of his classmates were listening but he persevered nonetheless.

When he had finished talking, Ms Joyce told him to pass the microscope around the class so that all the other children could have a closer look at it. But Sebastian replied that the item was very delicate, so, if she didn't mind, he'd rather not.

"You must share!" a child shouted.

"Don't be so selfish!" another said.

Ms Joyce walked over to Sebastian's desk and picked up the microscope. She gave it to Chantelle, and asked her to pass it along when she was finished looking at it. "What's this funny thing?" Chantelle asked as she pulled at the microscope's mirror.

"Please be careful…" Sebastian pleaded. He tried to keep track of his possession as it was being passed about the room. Suddenly, there was a clatter as someone dropped the microscope on the ground. Sebastian groaned. When the apparatus was eventually handed back to him, the mirror was cracked and the eye piece had been broken off. He was fuming but he decided to say nothing and just put the damaged item back into his schoolbag.

Ms Joyce told Adam that he could now go ahead and perform his 'Show and Tell'. Adam rummaged around in his bag for a few minutes and then reported to the teacher that he couldn't find the item he had brought with him; or at least, he thought he had brought with him. In retrospect, he must have accidently left it at home.

"Good call," Sebastian whispered and gave Adam a wink. Ms Joyce then looked to David, but he said he desperately had to go to the toilet and rushed out of the room. Ms Joyce proceeded to ask the remaining students who had brought an object with them to show and tell about it. The exhibited objects included plastic toys, make-up kits, jewellery, tattoo transfers, and laser pointers. Neither Sebastian nor Adam found any of the items particularly stimulating, but politely feigned interest as they were passed around.

At lunchtime, all the children at the school went to the canteen. Sebastian ordered an apple pie, Adam ordered a beef burger, while David ordered a salad bowl. After they had been given their food, they sat down at a table and Sebastian began to assess the damage done to the microscope. It seemed that both the eyepiece and the mirror would need to be replaced. The boys each agreed that they felt discouraged with their new school. It was so different from their last school, and Ms Joyce appeared to be the polar opposite of their old teachers in every way. The food they had just ordered tasted so bad that they couldn't eat it all. But they chatted for a while longer, and just as Adam was beginning to tell his friends about a victory that one of his father's horses had had in a race, Tyrone suddenly appeared. He put his plate of fried chicken down on their table and burst into a tirade, demanding to know why the boys only ever talked to each other and why seemed to think they were better than everybody else.

The boys tried to reassure Tyrone that they didn't think that they were better than everyone else, but he continued to quarrel with them and it was soon clear that he couldn't be placated. The boys stood up and headed for the door. Tyrone followed after, and continued to beleaguer them as they walked down the corridor. Sebastian began to feel agitated. He looked at his watch. There was still another half an hour before they had to go back to class. So he decided to pay a visit to the school library to try to find some quality reading material. He excused himself, and told David and Adam that he'd see them back in class.

Sebastian walked quickly to the school's reception area.

"Hey again buddy," Andy said when he saw him coming.

"Could you tell me where the library is please?" Sebastian asked.

"Yeah, course mate. It's in the green prefab building near the school car park. The librarian's name is Ms Bishop."

"Thank you very much," Sebastian said, and headed for the school's front doors.

"No worries mate," Andy replied. A blustery wind began to blow as Sebastian walked across the car park, whipping up some crisp bags from the ground.

Inside the library, a queue of children was slowing snaking its way towards Ms Bishop, who was sitting at a desk. Ms Bishop was a heavily-built woman with black wavy hair. She was laughing and joking with the boy standing at her desk, and seemed to have a bubbly, larger-than-life personality. Sebastian had a quick look around the library, but the only books on display and on the shelves were various editions of *Moral Stories for Kids*. However, he was in the mood for reading a novel, and so he joined the queue, intending to ask Ms Bishop if she could have a look in storage. There were three children in front of him, and within a few minutes two more had joined behind.

Sebastian waited patiently, and when his turn came, Ms Bishop gestured in his direction. He was about to step forward when the child standing directly behind him in the queue casually walked past him and strolled up to Ms

Bishop's desk. It was Tyrone! Sebastian was certain that Ms Bishop would tell Tyrone to return to his place in the queue as he was next. But much to his consternation, she started to smile and chat with Tyrone, and then began to check-out his books. "*Perhaps she didn't notice that I was next*," Sebastian thought to himself.

When Tyrone and Ms Bishop had finished their dealings, Ms Bishop once more gestured in Sebastian's direction. Yet again, the child standing directly behind Sebastian walked around him and over to Ms Bishop. It was Naomi, Tyrone's sister! Feeling bewildered, Sebastian walked briskly up to the librarian's desk.

"Sorry to interrupt, but I believe that I was next in the queue," he said politely.

"Just wait your turn please," Ms Bishop replied cuttingly.

Sebastian hesitated for a moment and then walked back to where he had been standing. Naomi and Ms Bishop chatted and giggled for a few minutes as Ms Bishop stamped her books.

When Naomi left, Ms Bishop looked towards Sebastian with an expression of contempt on her face. He walked over to her desk nervously and told her that he wasn't able to find the book he was looking for, but hoped that there might be a copy in storage.

"Okay, what's the name of book?" the hitherto jovial Ms Bishop asked nonchalantly.

"*Divide and Rule*," Sebastian replied.

Ms Bishop sighed and agreed to look in storage. She rose from her desk, waddled across the library floor and into a back room. A few minutes later she returned carrying a softcover book in her hand.

"You're in luck," she said. Ms Bishop proceeded to stamp the inside cover of the book and then handed it to him.

Sebastian thanked the librarian for her help, but she didn't respond.

As Sebastian made his way back across the car park towards the main school building, he wondered why Ms Bishop had been so unfriendly towards him. "*She must have heard bad things about me from Ms Joyce*," he assumed. Back in the classroom, Sebastian sat down at his desk beside Adam and David, and the class began their daily maths lesson. Just as the boys were expecting, Ms Joyce started writing simple sums on the whiteboard. She then asked Austin to calculate the answers, or if he found that too difficult, to just guess. Sebastian discretely took out from his bag a maths book that he brought with him from home (the one he'd used at his last school), and began to work on some algebra problems. But Ms Joyce saw what he was doing and immediately confiscated the book.

"Swot!", "Nerd!" some children shouted.

Sebastian murmured and put his head down. He and his two friends sat through the rest of the lesson feeling frustrated. At three o'clock, Ms Joyce set the homework assignment, which was again to provide an opinion of the stories covered in class that day.

At home that evening, Sebastian once more told his parents how Ms Joyce wouldn't tolerate any criticism of the moral stories, and how she forced him to study easy mathematics that he already knew. And now even the school librarian seemed to hate him. But worst of all, the other children in the class had broken his microscope. Mr and Mrs Howard again promised him that if the situation didn't improve in the near future, they would organise a meeting with his teacher.

* * *

The weeks went by, and Sebastian, Adam, and David gradually adapted to the routine in their new school. The bulk of the schoolwork consisted of reading and maths, with lesser focus on geography, history, science, computers, and art. And the foreign language taught was Arabic! The boys rarely learnt anything worthwhile that they didn't already know (although they regarded Arabic lessons as mildly interesting, they found it difficult to understand the strange letters). Also, Ms Joyce would spend a considerable amount of time each day attending to Austin as he had temper tantrums, adding to their frustrations.

As Sebastian and his two friends were amongst the most literate children in the class, Ms Joyce regularly called on them (and a handful of other children) to read the moral stories in their schoolbooks aloud, although she almost never asked them to *explain* the morals. Every day, the homework was always the same; simply to state one's opinion(s) of the stories covered that day in class. So this at least afforded the boys the opportunity to say what they really thought.

As the food from the canteen usually tasted terrible, Sebastian, David, and Adam began secretly smuggling items of food into school, keeping them hidden in their pockets until lunchtime. Although the boys had gotten to know some of their fellow students, there were so many children in the class that they still hadn't learned all their names.

Much to Sebastian and Adam's discontentment, David had become close to the flame-haired Becky. In fact, he was beginning to spend more time associating with her than with them. But Adam and Sebastian had taken an intense dislike to their friend's new companion. She was the type of girl who liked to find out as much as she could about a person, and then gossip about them to everybody else.

The boys had also learnt the names of some of the other teachers and staff members at the school. There was Mr Hays, a silver-haired man with glasses and a pointy nose; Mr Balls, a stout man with short brown hair; Ms Jackson, a plump, stony-faced woman; Ms Cooper, a ditzy young woman with short blonde hair; and Ms Mills, a cranky old lady who stalked the school corridors. Sebastian and Adam jokingly referred to the latter as the "the witch". There was also the bursar, Mr Darlington, who oversaw all financial matters at the school. He was a skinny, bespectacled man with big bushy eyebrows.

More concerning though, was a student called Nick. Nick was the school's main bully, and although he wasn't in their class, the boys would regularly see him in the playground or sometimes loitering in the school's hallways. He was short, stocky and cross-eyed, and he liked to glower at people intimidatingly. Students and teachers alike gave him a wide berth.

* * *

At home, the Howards were struggling to make ends meet as they ran down their savings. The economy remained in recession and the government had adopted the euro as the nation's new currency; everyone was still getting to grips with it. Due to their financial woes, Sebastian's parents sold their expensive cars and purchased a cheap, second-hand car for use between them. Mr Howard continued to attend the local Jobcentre and eventually accepted the only work he was offered: a low-paid job packing supermarket shelves. For the first time since Sebastian could remember, his father began working conventional working hours, usually getting home early each evening. Sensing his parents' distress, Sebastian took it upon himself to do more chores around the house (such as tidying, washing up, etc.).

Eventually, Sebastian and Adam began getting the bus to and from school each day as their mothers were finding the school run too expensive. They would alight at the stop outside the rehabilitation centre and then walk the remainder of the way. However, their parents made them promise never to wander off around the city by themselves, as it wasn't a safe place for children.

Due to an explosion in crime, most of city's residents now lived under a self-imposed curfew, rarely venturing outdoors after nightfall. 'Wanted' posters started appearing on lampposts throughout the city streets, but to Sebastian and his friends' surprise, most of the individuals in the photographs looked very clean-cut and respectable. They included employers who had discriminated against job applicants, police officers who had repeatedly stopped and searched known hooligans, and landlords who evicted tenants that didn't pay their rent. Television programmes would often be interrupted by news flashes stating that there had been an alleged sighting of a wanted individual. Viewers who spotted them, or who had any information as to their whereabouts, were urged to call the police. When an individual was apprehended, they were quickly put on trial and usually sentenced to a period of incarceration in the rehabilitation centre.

The governing regime continued to implement new rules and regulations, including more and more anti-discrimination legislation, red tape for businesses, an open-door immigration policy, and additional rights for minority groups. It also introduced a plethora of politically-correct speech codes, in an attempt to stifle all debate about its policies (the party's official line was that all the politically-correct terminology existed to prevent peoples' feelings getting hurt!). Now simply saying or doing things that other people found offensive were grounds for arrest.

* * *

Each evening, Sebastian continued to tell his parents that he felt frustrated at school and that his teacher and fellow students would get annoyed with him every time he expressed an opinion they didn't agree with. The couple finally agreed to have a meeting with Ms Joyce to discuss their son's concerns. Mrs Howard rang the school and scheduled the meeting for the three o'clock the following day. Sebastian's father managed to organise time off work so that he could attend also.

* * *

The next morning at breakfast, Sebastian felt cheerful for the first time since he had started at his new school. As he ate a bowl of cereal, he casually leafed through the morning papers that his father had left lying on the kitchen table. An article about the rehabilitation centre caught his eye. He read down through the piece, which reported that the centre had won a prestigious award for its excellent work rehabilitating criminals. But Mrs Howard advised him to get a move on or he might miss his bus. So he hauled his schoolbag onto his back and headed for the bus stop.

That day at school, Sebastian just went with the flow. He didn't challenge anything Ms Joyce taught or complain when they spent hours helping Austin learn rudimentary maths concepts. During the lunch period he chatted with Adam, as David was too busy consorting with Becky. He also returned the book that he had borrowed from the library. Ms Bishop said nothing as he handed the book back to her. At the end of the school day, when all the other children headed for home, Sebastian stayed in the classroom.

As it happened, Chantelle was also staying late and the pair got talking. Sebastian told her that his parents were having a meeting with Ms Joyce and that he would go home with them when they were finished.

"Mick is meeting Ms Joyce today also!" Chantelle said.

Sebastian asked who Mick was, and Chantelle told him that he was her new dad.

"Hmmm," Sebastian murmured disapprovingly. He asked whether Mick, like his own father, had taken time off work to attend the meeting, but much to his bafflement Chantelle stated that he didn't have a job.

"Where does your family get its money from then?" he asked.

Chantelle shrugged her shoulders.

Meanwhile, Mr and Mrs Howard had just arrived at the school. Andy the secretary led them into the staffroom where the meeting with Ms Joyce was scheduled to take place. It turned out that Ms Joyce was just finishing up a meeting with someone else, and so Andy told the couple to have a seat at the back of the room until she was ready to talk to them. The man Ms Joyce was talking to was wearing a red tracksuit and trainers. It was obvious that he was quite agitated, as he kept raising his voice and using expletives. But Sebastian's parents just stared at the floor, politely pretending that they hadn't noticed the unfolding drama.

The man suddenly grabbed Ms Joyce by the collar of her blouse and pulled her face up close to his. "I don't want you to correct my daughter ever again, understand?" he growled. He then made a rude hand gesture and barged out of the staffroom.

Ms Joyce just stood by her desk looking ruffled and a single tear ran down her cheek. But she quickly collected herself and invited the Howards over.

"I hope everything is alright?" Mr Howard asked with concern.

"Everything is fine, really," Ms Joyce said with a forced smile. "Now let's all have a seat and talk about Sebastian."

They all sat down, and Sebastian's parents explained to the teacher that their son was unhappy with his school texts and the fact that she wouldn't allow him study at a level more befitting to his ability. In addition, he didn't like that fact that she filmed the children as they explained the morals of the stories in their books, and this was something that they, as parents, also had a problem with. But Ms Joyce informed the Howards that they had actually given their consent for her to film Sebastian. She produced one of the forms that they had filled in when enrolling him in the school. And sure enough, in tiny print at the very bottom of the page, was a passage that stated that all children in the school would be filmed while explaining the moral values. It further stated that the resultant video clips would be sent to the rehabilitation centre for the purposes of teaching moral values to the inmates. Apparently, Mr and Mrs Howard had overlooked this when completing the form. The couple squabbled with Ms Joyce for a few minutes regarding the issue, but she assured them that once a form had been completed and signed, there was no going back.

In turn, Ms Joyce informed the Howards that she had some concerns of her own about their son; namely that he didn't seem to fit in with the other children and kept challenging everything she tried to teach him.

"Is it possible that he could be bored at school?" Mr Howard asked.

"No, not at all. Sebastian just needs to stop questioning everything and he will be fine," she replied.

"Well, is it possible that he needs a more advanced curriculum?" Sebastian's mother wondered.

Ms Joyce again said that if Sebastian would just stop questioning everything he would be fine. Ms Joyce's dull, monotonous demeanour was beginning to irritate Sebastian's parents, but they were too well-mannered to let their irritation show. They chatted with her about their son for a few more minutes, and then, when the meeting was finished, they thanked her for her time and shook her hand.

"Well that was a waste of time..." Mr Howard whispered discretely to his wife as they left. The couple collected Sebastian from his classroom and the trio left for home.

As soon as they had gone, Ms Joyce immediately picked up the telephone. She suspected that Sebastian was being mistreated by his parents. She couldn't put her finger on why she suspected this. There certainly wasn't any evidence to support the assertion, but Ms Joyce knew that gut feelings are more important than "facts" or "evidence". And so she did the only reasonable thing she felt she could do in this situation. She rang social services. By the time Sebastian and his parents arrived back at their house, there were two women waiting on the doorstep.

"I wonder who they are," Mr Howard enquired to his wife as they pulled into the driveway.

Mrs Howard replied that she didn't recognise them and didn't know who they were.

"Hello" the couple said in a friendly tone as they approached the two women. But the ladies just looked at them blankly and didn't return the salutation. "We are from social services and we want to talk to you about your son, Sebastian," one of them said.

The Howards felt a bit rattled, but nonetheless invited the two social workers inside. They had never had any dealings with social services before, but had heard many horror stories about them. The social workers stayed in the house for hours, questioning Sebastian and his parents about every minute detail of their lives. One social worker even took out a measuring tape and measured Sebastian. It transpired that he was below average height for a boy his age, and she wondered aloud whether this might be as a result of malnourishment. Sebastian's parents could feel their blood begin to boil. What annoyed them the most was the social workers' passive-agressive approach. They spoke in a very calm, sickly-sweet manner while insinuating that the Howards were bad parents. However, the Howards knew better than to show any outwards signs of anger, as the social workers might use it against them.

One of the social workers knelt down beside Sebastian. "Tell me, have you made many friends at your new school?"

"Not really," Sebastian answered, rubbing the back of his neck with his hand.

"And do you ever find it difficult to stay focused on your schoolwork?" was her next question.

"Yes, all the time!" he replied. "The stories in our schoolbooks are really stupid and boring – I hate them! And when we study other subjects like maths, history, or geography, I never learn anything new." The woman made some notes in her notepad.

When they were finally finished asking questions, the social workers told Mr and Mrs Howard that they had some concerns. They noted that Sebastian's music CDs and books were very archaic, and said it was a proven fact that traditional folktales can be very frightening for children. Hence, they advised the Howards to buy their son some more contemporary reading and listening material. In addition, they recommended that Sebastian no longer be required to complete chores around the house, as doing so infringed too much on his personal freedom. They also said that it was possible that Sebastian's excessive dislike of school, especially his hatred of the stories in his schoolbooks, might be due to a mental disorder, and advised that he see a psychologist for a clinical evaluation.

The social workers gave Sebastian's parents the phone number of the local mental health clinic and insisted that an appointment be made for Sebastian before they left. The two social workers stood beside Mrs Howard, continuing to make notes as she reluctantly picked up the telephone and began to dial. The secretary at the clinic who took the call said that the waiting list was very long, but as it happened there had just been a cancellation for nine o'clock the next morning. Mrs Howard agreed to take the slot.

The social workers said that they wished to be informed of the outcome of the psychological assessment. If it turned out that Sebastian didn't have a mental disorder, they would need to continue their evaluation of his home life. Once the two social workers had completed their paperwork, and ticked all the applicable boxes, they left. Later that evening, Sebastian's mother went to the local shops and bought some hip-hop CDs and teen magazines. It wasn't that she intended for her son to make use of them; rather, it was just to appease the social workers if they ever came to call again.

CHAPTER 5

Sebastian felt nervous about seeing a psychologist, but was glad to have the day off school. The mental health clinic was on the other side of the city, and as her husband had the car that day, Mrs Howard decided that they would get the train. The station was bustling and Sebastian held his mother's hand tightly so that they wouldn't become separated. They bought tickets and waited on the platform amongst the throngs of commuters. Sebastian began to feel a bit claustrophobic when a group of young men wearing bulky backpacks began squashing against him. He tried his best to ignore them, but couldn't so he walked closer to the edge of the platform for a bit of breathing space.

On the rusty railway tracks below, he noticed rats and mice scurrying about in the shadows. When the train arrived (five minutes late), everyone got on board. Sebastian and his mother walked through the carriages looking for free seats. Unable to find two side by side, they sat directly across from each other.

Sebastian found himself sitting next to two businessmen who were immersed in conversation. They were both dressed in blue suits and wore red ties, and each had with them a briefcase and laptop. The men were eating noodles and rice from a carton, and kept squinting as the yellow morning sun shone through the carriage windows directly onto their faces. One of the men caught Sebastian staring at him and gave him a friendly smile.

"You two are eating dinner very early!" Sebastian said with a chuckle.

The businessmen laughed heartily. "This really is our dinner!" one of them replied. "We've just arrived in the city after a 10 hour flight and are now heading to a very important business meeting."

"That's very interesting," Sebastian said. "I'm going to see a psychologist because I might have a mental problem."

"Oh..." the man replied, and started fiddling with his chopsticks.

A few moments of awkward silence ensued.

"*I wish I hadn't said that*," Sebastian thought.

The train had only travelled a short distance when, without warning, it began to vibrate and then ground to a complete halt.

Everybody was unsure what was happening, and some passengers became visibly anxious. But after a few minutes, the train driver walked through the carriages and reassured everyone that it was just a mechanical issue. He added that engineers were working on the problem and that they should be on their way again soon. But 20 minutes later, the train remained stationary on the tracks. The atmosphere was becoming very stuffy and so some passengers pried open the carriage's sliding doors. Sebastian and his mother followed the rest of the commuters out onto the scrubland alongside the railway tracks. Two engineers wearing orange overalls were working at the front of the train. They had opened a metal hatch and were examining some of the vehicle's internal mechanisms. The commuters began to gather around and prompted the two men to hurry up.

Sebastian looked at his watch and started growing concerned that if the problem wasn't sorted out soon he would miss his appointment with the psychologist. The businessman who had chatted to Sebastian walked over to the engineers and asked if he could have a look. They inquired whether he was a qualified train mechanic, but the man replied that he was not.

"Then I'm afraid we can't let you anywhere near the train's engine," one of them said curtly.

"Oh, just let me have a look or we'll be here all day," the businessman replied, pushing past the engineers. He began fiddling around with various knobs and levers, and after a few minutes he announced that he had fixed the problem. All the passengers cheered with great excitement. The engineers in the orange overalls then carefully inspected the work, and in an attempt to avoid losing face, told the crowd that they had sorted out the problem. All the passengers cheered once again and climbed back onto the train.

As Sebastian sat back down, he looked out through the fogged-up carriage window and saw the businessman still chatting to the two engineers. The businessman then embarked and took his seat. He leaned up close to his colleague and began to whisper to him. Sebastian pretended that he was just daydreaming out the window, but secretly strained to hear what was being said. "... and the frightening thing is, they both have university degrees." Grins appeared on both men's faces and their eyes narrowed into little slits.

"Well then, let's just hope our associates at the business meeting went to the same university as those clowns!" The two businessmen burst into laughter.

The train shuttled forward again. After a few minutes Sebastian's mother waved over at him, indicating that they would be getting off at the next platform. When the train stopped they alighted and walked up a short flight of concrete steps to the city streets. Sebastian and his mother carefully followed the street signs until they located the clinic. It was situated within an ugly grey high-rise building, at the front of which was a bronze statue of a stern-looking man sitting on a rock, with his hands on his hips. It was just after nine o'clock when the pair rang the bell to the side of the building's front door. The receptionist answered and invited them in. She led them up a flight of stairs to an office and introduced them to the psychologist, Mr Maxwell; a mild-mannered old man with spectacles and a shock of white hair.

He made some casual small talk about the weather to help put the pair at ease. Mrs Howard told Mr Maxwell that she was pleased that he could see Sebastian so soon, albeit because somebody else had cancelled their appointment. She said she knew that the waiting list to see health professionals was extremely long.

"Oh yes, the entire public health system in this country is an ungodly mess," Mr Maxwell replied. "In fact, I am currently writing a paper that blows the whistle on all the corruption," he continued as he sat down on his armchair and leaned back. "But enough about that, let's talk about young Sebastian."

Mrs Howard explained that her son was having difficulty fitting in in his new school, and that his teacher felt that he was too critical of everything she tried to teach him.

Mr Maxwell nodded along empathetically. He said that after he conducted he psychological evaluation of Sebastian today, he would know for certain whether he suffered from a mental disorder or not. Mrs Howard asked the psychologist about the tests he planned to use in his clinical assessment, but Mr Maxwell said that he wouldn't be using any tests. Rather, he would just be talking to her son. As Sebastian was so young, Mr Maxwell said that he was happy for Mrs Howard to be present while he conducted the psychological evaluation. With that, he told Sebastian to lie down on the couch and relax. "Tell me about your mother..." Mr Maxwell said. Sebastian told the psychologist that his mummy was very nice and that they got on very well together. "And sometimes you get jealous because you think she loves your father more than you, don't you?"

"No," Sebastian replied.

Mr Maxwell sustained this line of questioning and asked Sebastian whether he ever feels that his mother doesn't love him enough. Mrs Howard began to feel very uncomfortable at the way Mr Maxwell kept talking about her as if she was some sort of cold, unloving monster. But she reasoned that as a qualified and state registered psychologist, he must know what he's doing.

"How do you find school?" Mr Maxwell then asked, changing the subject.

"Boring! Sebastian replied. "The stories in my schoolbooks teach very immoral lessons, and the whole class is forced to continue doing very basic sums just because one boy in the class is weak at maths."

"And have you told your teacher how you feel?" Mr Maxwell enquired.

"Yes, I've challenged her about these issues many times, but she doesn't listen to a word I say!" Sebastian told him.

Mr Maxwell nodded. "Based on what you've told me, I'd imagine that you must find it difficult to pay attention at school?"

"*Very* difficult" Sebastian said, feeling relieved to be getting his grievances off his chest to someone who seemed to care. Mr Maxwell continued to chat with Sebastian for another 10 minutes, and at the end of the session he informed Mrs Howard that her son did indeed suffer from not one, but two mental disorders – Oppositional Defiant Disorder and Attention Deficit Disorder. He said that the conditions would need to be treated with medication but that the pills could only be provided by a medical doctor, so they would need to obtain a prescription from their physician.

Sebastian and his mother thanked Mr Maxwell for all his help as they left the clinic. On the way home, they stopped at their GP's surgery and duly obtained a prescription for the medication that Mr Maxwell had recommended. They then collected the medication from a local pharmacy.

As soon as they arrived home, Mrs Howard rang her son's school and clued Ms Joyce in about the visit to the psychologist. She told her about Sebastian's diagnoses and informed her that he had been prescribed medication. Ms Joyce said that she wasn't at all surprised that Sebastian had mental problems, as she had long suspected that there was something wrong with him.

"I'd appreciate it if you didn't mention his diagnoses to any of the other children in the class," Mrs Howard requested of her. "I'd worry that it might go against him in the future."

"I'm afraid school policy stipulates that all the students are to be informed if a classmate has a psychological problem – they have the right to know," was Ms Joyce's response.

"Okay, I see. Goodbye Ms Joyce," Mrs Howard said as she hung up the phone, annoyed by the teacher's stubbornness. She then rang the social workers that had visited them and dutifully told them of the psychologist's diagnoses. They said they would need a copy of Mr Maxwell's report and, if verified, they would discontinue their investigation of the family.

Sebastian poured himself a glass of water and dutifully took his medication. He didn't notice any difference at first, but after half an hour he felt like a zombie. Everything became dreamlike and he found it difficult to think straight. He just sat in a chair staring blankly at the television. Mrs Howard became very concerned and rang Mr Maxwell. However, the psychologist informed her that her son's reaction to the medication was completely normal and that there was nothing to worry about. When Sebastian's father returned from work, he too was baffled by his son's zombie-like state. However, they just hoped that Sebastian would return to normal once his body became accustomed to the drug.

* * *

At school the next day, Ms Joyce asked David to read out a story called *Larry the Looter.*

> *Larry smashed his way through the window of a sports shop and helped himself to money from the till and some new sportswear. As he was trashing the shop, a security man suddenly yelled, "Freeze!" Larry spun around and the security man could see the frustration in his eyes.*
>
> *"I'm unemployed, I can't pay my bills and my ex-girlfriend keeps hassling me for child support," Larry said sorrowfully. "Wouldn't any person in my position act the way I act?"*
>
> *"Hmm, I'd never thought of it that way – I suppose you're right," the security man replied, and sympathetic towards Larry's plight, he handed him some banknotes from his pocket and sent him on his way.*

When David had finished, Ms Joyce addressed the class. "Now kids, Sebastian has recently been diagnosed with mental problems..."

"Huh?" Adam blurted out.

"But his opinions are just as valid as anybody else's so we should all listen to what he has to say." She then looked directly at Sebastian and asked him to come up the front of the room and explain the moral of the story. Sebastian shuffled towards the teacher in a psychotropic stupor and stood by her desk. Sebastian knew that the story David had just read was silly, but his medication had him feeling placid, and he was in no mood to argue with his teacher. It would be easier to just tell her what she wanted to hear. When Ms Joyce pointed her video camera at him, he began to speak slowly and with a slight slur.

"When people are unemployed and can't afford to pay bills or child support, etc., it's only to be expected that they'll sometimes loot shops and smash everything up in frustration. We shouldn't be too quick to judge such people."

Ms Joyce looked delighted. "Well done Sebastian! Well done!" she said. All the children in the class, except Adam and David began to clap. Ms Joyce reached into her handbag, pulled out a bar of chocolate and handed it to Sebastian.

"When were you diagnosed with mental problems?" Adam asked his friend as he sat back down.

"Yesterday" Sebastian replied. "A nice psychologist told me I have Oppositional Defiant Disorder and Attention Deficit Disorder, and I got put on medication."

"What on earth are Oppositional Defiant Disorder and Attention Deficit Disorder?" David asked.

"I think it means that I won't cooperate at school and don't stay focused on my schoolwork," Sebastian informed him as he chomped on his chocolate.

"Hmmm" said Adam, not quite sure what to make of his friend's diagnoses.

At break-time, the boys went to the canteen and Sebastian mindlessly watched daytime television as he ate his lunch. Adam and David tried to converse with him, but couldn't because he just kept staring expressionlessly at the TV screen. Becky came over to join them and started asking Sebastian about his mental problems. "Does it mean you're mad?", "Are you dangerous?", "Do you hear voices in your head?"

"No, I don't think so…" was his response to each question.

When class resumed, Sebastian sat patiently as Ms Joyce taught maths to Austin, before she moved onto an Arabic lesson, and then computers. At the end of the school day, Ms Joyce said that she had seen a huge improvement in Sebastian and that she was very happy with him.

When he arrived home that afternoon, he immediately went about completing his homework. He wrote that "The stories we read in class today were wonderful!"

"*That should keep Ms Joyce happy*," he thought. But by late evening, Sebastian was beginning to feel prickly. He didn't like the way he couldn't think straight when he was medicated. When it was time for him to take his medication again, he told his mother that he didn't want to take any more pills. Concerned about the effect they had on her son, Mrs Howard agreed that it might be best if he discontinued taking them, and instead gave him a toasted cheese sandwich and a glass of milk.

Within a few hours, Sebastian's personality had returned to normal, much to the delight of his parents. As he lay in bed that night, Sebastian simmered as he thought about how the world seemed to be turning against him. He began to thump his pillow in frustration and fantasised that it was Ms Joyce. Then he froze in horror when he realised what he was doing. This wasn't like him at all. For a moment, he wondered whether he really was starting to go mad.

* * *

By the next morning, Sebastian had decided that, come hell or high water, he was going to challenge the stories in his schoolbooks. In fact, he wouldn't cease until every child in his class knew how preposterous they were. He confided in Adam and David that he had stopped taking medication for his mental disorders, but insisted that they must not tell anyone else. When Ms Joyce arrived into class, she looked at Sebastian with a big smile. She said that his behaviour in class yesterday was exemplary, so today she would like him to explain the morals of some new stories they were going to read. The first story up was *Nurse Nancy* and Ms Joyce selected a student called Greg to read it aloud. Greg was a fairly nondescript boy with short brown hair. He wore a pair of blue jeans and a sweatshirt emblazoned with a picture of a flying yellow bird. Ms Joyce assisted him as he read.

> *Nurse Nancy worked in the city hospital. She knew from her training that compassion and a non-discriminatory attitude is what makes a good nurse. Therefore, Nancy always attended to her patients in a random order, paying no heed to the nature of their ailments. One Saturday night a drunken man named Ashley burst into A&E and began threatening all the other patients with a knife. But compassionate as she was, Nancy knew that Ashley's rage was a direct measure of how unfairly he had been treated by society. And so she dashed past a victim of a stabbing who had just been brought in by paramedics and attended to the disadvantaged Ashley first.*

When Greg was finished, Sebastian strolled confidently up to the teacher's desk. Ms Joyce pointed her camera at him and gave a nod. "Nurse Nancy was a stupid story. Ashley was a total lowlife and Nancy should have attended to the stabbing victim first," he declared in an uncharacteristically cocky tone.

All the children in the class began to look at each other with shocked expressions on their faces and Ms Joyce reacted by throwing her arms up in despair.

"Remember kids, Sebastian has mental problems so don't take anything he says too seriously!" she said, and then told him to return to his seat.

"I'm glad you've come back to your senses," Adam whispered as his friend sat back down.

Sebastian continued to pipe up throughout the day, pointing out the absurdity of each story the class read. He was aware that Ms Joyce and his fellow students were becoming increasingly agitated by his criticisms.

"Shut up!" Greg kept telling him.

Even David eventually urged him to quieten down. Sebastian didn't let any of this bother him, but when he returned home that afternoon, Mrs Howard told him that Ms Joyce had rung and said that he had been very challenging at school today. She wanted to know if he had taken his medication that morning and said that if his behaviour didn't improve by tomorrow she would ring the social workers and ask them to investigate. Sebastian could see that his mother was very upset, so he decided that it might be best to play along at school for the foreseeable future.

CHAPTER 6

One Monday morning, as Sebastian and Adam alighted from their bus, they noticed their former headmaster, Mr Stevens, walking up the steps at the entrance to the rehabilitation centre. They were excited to see him again and called over to him. Naturally enough, the boys asked why he was going into the centre. Mr Stevens told them that he had applied for a job there and was going to attend an interview. Sebastian said that he had heard good things about the centre and read in the newspaper it had won an award.

But a serious expression appeared on Mr Stevens face and he leant down towards the boys. "The truth is that the rehabilitation centre is a dreadful place," he said. "People come out worse than they went in." Feeling perplexed, Adam asked him why he wanted to work there then. "I'll tell you a secret if you promise not to tell anyone," Mr Stevens replied, looking back over his shoulder to make sure no one could overhear. The boys promised that they wouldn't tell a soul. Mr Stevens leaned right down and whispered. "If I can get a job working here, maybe I can bring it down from the inside." Sebastian asked what was so bad about the rehabilitation centre that he wanted to "bring it down", but Mr Stevens didn't seem to want to discuss it anymore.

"Enough about me," he said. "How are things going at your new school?" Not wanting to appear to be badmouthing their new school to their former headmaster, the boys told him that things were "fine" but that they were still settling in.

"Yes, of course," Mr Steven's said. Sebastian then mentioned that he had been to see a psychologist and had been diagnosed with two mental disorders. Mr Stevens was taken aback by this news and told Sebastian that he had always seemed completely normal to him. But at any rate, Mr Stevens was pressed for time. He looked at his watch and said that he had better get going as he didn't want to be late for his interview. They parted ways and Adam and Sebastian continued on to school.

They managed to arrive on time, and just as they were sitting down at their desks, Ms Joyce asked Sebastian to go to the school caretaker's office and get some oil for the rusty hinge on the window latch. So off he went down the corridor and searched around until he eventually located the office.

The door was already open so he went inside. The walls of the room were caked in grime and a filthy red mat lay on the floor. And there, sitting at a table in the middle of the office, was a little man with a bald head and a scruffy, grey beard. He was a reading a thick, hardcover book and eating a kebab.

The man looked up as Sebastian walked towards him. "Hello, I'm Mr McHugh, the school caretaker," he said in a rather gruff tone. "And this is Sam," he added, pointing to a black cat sitting in the corner of the room, silently lapping up milk from a saucer. Sam briefly glanced over at Sebastian, revealing a little moustache of milk on his snout.

"I haven't seen you before. Are you a new student?" Mr McHugh asked.

"Yes. I used to attend a private school, but when the government closed it, I came here," Sebastian said.

"You're much better off here," Mr McHugh told him as he took a bite on his kebab. "You won't find any middle class snobbery at this school," he added, talking with his mouth full. "How are you finding it so far?"

"Well, I find it all a bit strange to be honest. Particularly the fact that there are no exams."

Mr McHugh rubbed his furry chin and laughed. "That's right. It's your indefatigability that's important, not some stupid test score."

"What does *in-de-fat-ig-ability* mean?" Sebastian asked, trying to sound out the big word.

"It's impossible to define," Mr McHugh replied.

Sebastian told the caretaker that Ms Joyce had sent him to get some oil for the rusty hinge on the classroom window. Mr McHugh rummaged around the office for a few minutes until he eventually found a small can with a pointed nozzle. Just as he handed it to Sebastian, a clatter echoed throughout the room as Sam the cat dashed along the shelves, knocking over cans filled with turpentine and paint.

"Sam!!!" Mr McHugh yelled, and began chasing after the feline.

Back in his classroom, Sebastian gave the can of oil to Ms Joyce and then took his seat. The class got straight into reading their moral stories. Sebastian, Adam and David had long since given up challenging Ms Joyce about them, and whenever she called on one of them to explain the moral of a story, they just said what they knew she wanted to hear.

After covering some maths and a simple science lesson, the day ended with a fire drill – but it didn't go smoothly. Most of the children in class laughed at Ms Joyce as she tried to escort them towards the door, and failed to follow her instructions.

For the first time in his life, Sebastian hated school. In fact, he had begun to live for the weekends.

* * *

One Saturday afternoon, Sebastian was over at Adam's house. Adam's mother was vacuuming, while his father was upstairs doing some business-related paperwork. As the two boys were munching on some of Mrs Smith's cookies, they decided to play a game of Scrabble. They went into the drawing room and Adam took his Scrabble set out from a cabinet drawer. After about half an hour of playing, the boys became vaguely aware of a rattling noise coming from the next room. However, they didn't think much of it, initially assuming that it was just Mrs Smith cleaning. Adam placed a few letters on the board, spelling out the word 'parable'. He totted up his score and then it was Sebastian's turn. Sebastian carefully checked his letters against those already on the board. Slowly, he added some new tiles to spell out 'indefatigability'. But Adam hadn't heard the big word before and asked what it meant. "It's impossible to define," Sebastian informed his friend.

"Are you sure about that?" Adam replied sceptically, brushing his fringe out of his eyes.

Just as they were about to go in search of a dictionary, a man wearing a long, black coat and a black fedora hat suddenly entered the room. The two boys looked at each other, stunned. The man was skinny and gaunt, and had a scraggly beard. The pupils of his eyes were dilated and he kept making strange jerking movements. He also stank of body odour.

"Where do you keep the money!?" he yelled, looking towards the boys.

Adam and Sebastian began to back away from the strange man. He again asked where the family kept their money, and then began riffling through the drawers in one of the drawing room's cabinets.

"Burglar!" Adam shouted, and moments later Mr and Mrs Smith rushed into the room.

Mrs Smith let out a shrill scream when she saw the man, while Adam's father stared at the intruder with an expression of terror on his face. The burglar looked towards the couple and snarled at them. He then lunged at Adam's father, and wrestled him to the ground. He thumped Mr Smith violently and then began to choke him. Adam's mother became hysterical and frantically tried to drag the burglar off her husband. Sebastian and Adam joined in, pulling the man by his legs.

The burglar and Mr Smith rolled around on the ground, exchanging punches. Mrs Smith ran into the hallway, and in a state of panic she picked up the telephone and rang the police. Meanwhile, Adam's father had managed to stagger over to the fireplace. He grabbed the poker and whacked the burglar over the head with it. The man crashed to the ground. He lay silently on the carpet for a few seconds, before beginning to groan.

As the burglar began to crawl across the floor, Sebastian and Adam leapt onto his back, pinning him down. Mr Smith frantically searched around the drawing room, and when he found a ball of twine, he tied the burglar's arms and legs together. The man struggled violently against his restraints. He began to scream obscenities, and kept saying that he knew his rights. The stream of vile language prompted Mr Smith to but a gag in his mouth. Adam's mother, still in a panicked state, came back into the drawing room and said the police were on their way. Everyone helped hold the burglar down, preventing him from wriggling away. Mr Smith told Sebastian to go and fetch his parents.

Sebastian ran the short distance back to his house and told his mother and father what had happened. The couple and their son hurried over to the Smiths' residence to see if they could be of any assistance. When they arrived, Mrs Smith was crying uncontrollably in the hallway and Sebastian's mother immediately went to comfort her. Sebastian and his father rushed into the drawing room, where Adam and Mr Smith were still sitting by the burglar, keeping him pinned to the ground. Mr Smith was clearly injured with a bruised face and a black eye, so Sebastian and his father offered him their assistance.

When it looked like the men and boys had the situation under control, Mrs Howard took Mrs Smith into the kitchen and made her a cup of tea to help calm her down. An hour and a half later, the police still hadn't arrived. Sebastian's mother rang them several times, but they just kept fobbing her off. Mr Howard said that the best thing to do under the circumstances would be to take the burglar to the police station themselves. And so, himself and Mr Smith carried the man out to Mr Smith's car and forced him in through the back door. He continued to squeal and struggle, but couldn't escape from his bonds. The two families agreed that they should all go to the police station together. And so the boys' respective fathers and the burglar set off in Mr Smith's car, while the two women and the boys followed behind in his wife's car.

They drove through the city and eventually arrived at the police station. Mr Smith and Sebastian's father led the burglar from the car and in through the front doors of the drab stone building. They undid his gag, and he immediately began shouting and swearing again. Several police officers ran over when they heard the commotion, and Mr Smith explained to them what had happened back at his house. As the burglar was becoming increasingly aggressive, the officers took him away to the cells. When they returned a few minutes later, they told the two families that they should leave now as they, the police, would take care of everything from that point on. But Mr and Mrs Smith demanded to speak to the sergeant in charge and so one of the policemen went to fetch him. When he finally appeared, the Smiths again reiterated about the break-in. But the sergeant seemed to be only half listening as they explained about how the burglar had attacked Mr Smith, and how they had then managed to subdue him and tie him up. By the end, it was clear that the sergeant was irritated.

He told the Smiths that they should not have resisted the burglar or restrained him, and said that they themselves could now potentially be charged with assault and false imprisonment. Mr Howard pointed out that if the police had actually bothered to show up when they were called, there would have been no need for them to restrain him. The sergeant looked disgusted. He then tried to talk the Smiths out of filing a report on the incident, noting that it would take a long time to complete all the necessary paperwork. But Adam's mother was very insistent that charges be pressed against the man, and after bickering with the police sergeant for 15 minutes, he caved in.

"Alright, fine..." he grumbled and led everyone to an office.

The four adults and two boys sat with the sergeant for several hours, arduously filling in dozens of forms. It was late in the evening when they left the police station.

They all went back to the Smiths' house, and Sebastian and his parents helped clean up the mess that had been made during the scuffle. Mrs Smith examined her husband's injuries, and urged him to see a doctor. He agreed to make an appointment in the morning. The Smiths thanked Sebastian and his parents for all their help, and as the Howards left, they told their friends that if they needed any further assistance to let them know. Back at their own home, Sebastian's father went around the house, double-checking that all the windows were closed and locked.

"It seems you can't be too careful these days," he said as he turned on the alarm.

* * *

At school the next day, as Sebastian and Adam were telling David about the incident with the burglar, Ms Joyce overheard the boys talking and asked what had happened. Adam explained how an intoxicated burglar had broken into his house and attacked his father. Then, when they brought him to the police station, the police officers put him in a cell and (after much haranguing) charged him with burglary and assault.

"It sounds like the police were very harsh on the poor man," Ms Joyce said pitifully.

As the boys continued to talk to their teacher, Mr Wallace's nasally voice sounded through the school's intercom system. He said that he had some very exciting news. He would be going on a fundraising outing today and was looking for some kids to accompany him. A photographer would come along to take pictures and there would be a write-up about the fundraising trip in a local newspaper. Mr Wallace went on to say that any students who were interested in coming along should leave their details with the school secretary. The winners would be chosen via a raffle. But there was even more thrilling news. A celebrity would be coming to visit the school later in the afternoon to help generate some publicity!

All the children in the class began to cheer and scream when they heard that a celebrity would be visiting them. Chantelle began flapping her hand in front of her face to prevent herself from fainting. Sebastian immediately decided to enter the competition. Anything to get away from Ms Joyce and those dreaded schoolbooks! Adam decided to enter also, but David said he was content to sit through the morning's lessons as he was really beginning to enjoy some of the moral stories. The two boys stood up and walked out of class. They made their way to the school reception area and joined the queue of children that was standing in front of Andy's desk. One by one, each child wrote their name on a scrap of paper and dropped it into a box on the reception desk. Once they had entered, Sebastian and Adam returned to class.

About 10 minutes into their moral lessons, Mr Wallace's voice again came over the intercom. He started calling out the names of the children who had been selected in the raffle. Sebastian heard his name being called and gave a little smile. But he was disappointed not to hear Adam's name. Sebastian made his way to the assembly area where the head teacher was standing chatting to a man with a camera. Gradually, a group of children began to form. Of the children in Sebastian's class, only two others had also been picked – Abdul and Greg. Mr Wallace began to brief the group. He said that they were going to walk through nearby housing estates, knocking on people's doors and asking for donations. He told the children that they didn't need to say anything as he would do all the talking.

And so the group set off on their long march. Of the residents who were at home, most were helpful and contributed towards the fundraiser. However, some said they couldn't spare any money, and one man even slammed the door in Mr Wallace's face. After about an hour and a half, Mr Wallace and the children had collected a considerable amount of coins and notes. Eventually they approached a mundane-looking semi-detached dwelling, and as just as the head teacher rang the doorbell, Greg said, "This is my house."

"Oh…" replied Mr Wallace.

A few seconds later Greg's mother answered the door and Mr Wallace explained to her that they were fundraising for their school. The woman kindly agreed to help them out, and took some coins from her purse and dropped them in the collection bucket.

Greg's mother then invited everyone inside for refreshments, but Mr Wallace declined the offer, saying that they were short on time. Just as the group was about to move on, Greg suddenly declared that there was something that he wanted to show everyone. He dashed past his mother and ran up the stairs.

"We really should get going," Mr Wallace mumbled, looking at his watch.

After a few seconds, Greg returned with a squirrel sitting on his shoulder. "This is Danny," he said. He explained that he had found Danny abandoned as a baby and had taken it upon himself to raise him. All the children giggled as Danny hopped about on Greg's shoulder and cautiously sniffed the air. They took turns petting the little ginger rodent, and Greg's mother urged Mr Wallace to join in. But the school head teacher said that he didn't like animals, or children for that matter, and stood well back.

The assemblage traipsed off down the street with Danny the squirrel riding along on his owner's shoulder. By now it was early afternoon, and Mr Wallace said that they would only have time to visit a couple more houses. He stared over at Abdul and looked him up and down.

"Where do you live?" he asked. When Abdul replied that his home was only a few streets away, Mr Wallace decided that they would pay a visit to Abdul's parents. Everyone trudged forwards again and when they eventually reached Abdul's house, Mr Wallace straightened his red tie and gave a knock at the door.

Within a few seconds, Abdul's mother answered.

"Hello! Is your husband home?" the head teacher asked.

"Yes," the woman confirmed. "He's in the kitchen having his lunch, but he'll be going back to work soon."

Mr Wallace enquired if they could come in, but Abdul's mother said the timing was a little inconvenient.

Suddenly, Abdul's father appeared in the hallway behind his wife. "Who is it dear?" he asked.

But before his wife had a chance to reply, Mr Wallace traipsed past her and into the house. "Come on in everyone" he said, beckoning the children and photographer inside. However, he told Greg to stay in the front garden with his pet squirrel. The head teacher extended his hand to Abdul's father and told him that they were fundraising for their school.

Abdul's dad looked stunned and was about to say something when Mr Wallace suddenly blurted out, "Oh, I should really take off my shoes." With that, he knelt down and began to undo his shoelaces. The photographer started to take pictures.

Abdul's mother rolled her eyes upwards. "There is no need for this. We don't even take off our own shoes when we come into the house."

But Mr Wallace just ignored her and continued imploring everyone to take their shoes off. He reached towards Sebastian. "Here, let me help you," he said, and began to pull Sebastian's shoes from his feet.

Abdul's mother was becoming irate. "Stop this madness," she kept saying. But Mr Wallace wasn't listening, and lumbered around the hallway, knocking over vases and ornaments in his desperate bid to get everyone to take off their shoes. Abdul's mum finally had enough and exploded in anger. "Why don't you actually listen to anything I tell you!?" she roared. The hallway fell silent. Mr Wallace looked embarrassed and his cheeks began to turn pink.

"Okay, let's, let's move along now kids," he stuttered. He pulled open the front door and walked outside, with the children and photographers following suit. It was beginning to rain now. Everyone pulled up their hoods and headed back towards the school.

When they arrived back, Mr Wallace and the children gathered in the bursar's office. The head teacher placed all the proceeds from the fundraiser onto a table. He and the bursar, Mr Darlington, gave big grins as the photographer snapped them holding thick wads of cash in their hands. By now it was the early afternoon, and staff and students alike were getting excited in anticipation of the impending celebrity visit.

Everyone made their way to the school playground as they waited for the famous person to arrive. As the throngs of children mucked about, Sebastian and Adam paced back and forth along the railings adjacent to the main road while David played rock-paper-scissors with Becky. A white van pulled up on the grass verge on the opposite side of the railings. 'Paul's Plumbing Service', it said in blue lettering on the van's side panelling.

The driver rolled down the window and shouted over to the children. "Hey kids, where's the main entrance to the school?"

Sebastian was about to point him towards the school gates when all the other children began chattering loudly. "Stranger… It's a stranger," they kept repeating.

Suddenly Chantelle yelled out "Mr Redmond! There's a strange man in a van over here bothering us." The van driver's face went white. Mr Redmond rushed over to the railings. He took his mobile phone out of his pocket and started to take pictures of the van and its occupant. The man quickly rolled up the window and van's engine revved loudly. Within seconds it had sped off down the road.

No sooner had the van left when the school gates opened and a shiny white limousine drove in. Mr Wallace dashed towards the vehicle. One of the limo's back doors opened and two cameramen got out. The children started to get hysterical, and suddenly a big cheer went up as the celebrity slowly climbed out from the limo. He was an older man, and wore a shellsuit and lots of gold jewellery. Sebastian recognised him from the television but didn't know his name. Adam and David didn't know either. The man started to make funny faces, causing the children to erupt into fits of giggling. Mr Wallace smirked as the cameramen took footage of the two of them shaking hands. They then walked into the school together, followed by hordes of excited children. The cameramen continued to film as the celebrity pulled a flute out of his trouser pocket and started to play a tune. He danced forward, his flowing locks trailing after him. A group of children joined together to form a human train behind the man, and another group interlocked their outstretched arms to form a tunnel, through which the train passed.

When everybody was finished dancing, the celebrity looked exhausted. "I need to use the bathroom," he said. But Mr Wallace informed him with regret that the toilet was broken. "We telephoned a plumber to come and have a look, but he still hasn't shown up."

"Well, maybe I can fix it?" the celebrity asked.

And so Mr Wallace led the man into the toilet cubical. He picked up a plunger from the floor, thrust it down the toilet, and then pulled it out again. He kept repeating this action for several minutes until he had managed to remove a blockage. "How's about that then!?" he said. All the teachers and children gave him a big clap.

"You don't mind if I have a smoke, do you?" the celebrity asked Mr Wallace as they made their way back into the assembly hall. The head teacher replied that normally people aren't allowed to smoke in the school building, but that they were happy to make an exception for him. The celebrity lit up a cigar, and several of the children began to cough in the ensuing clouds of smoke. The man spent several hours in the school, looking around and playing with the children. Eventually, it was time for him to leave. Mr Wallace thanked the man deeply for making the appearance.

"No problem. It's all for a good cause" he replied as the two of them again shook hands.

Cries of disappointment went up as the celebrity began to plod towards the school's exit. However, just before he left, he suddenly turned around and pulled another funny face! All the children burst into laughter.

CHAPTER 7

Soon the autumn gave way to winter. By now, most of the country's population lived in a constant state of paranoia, always fearful that they might offend someone and end up getting arrested. The Howards' financial situation had worsened considerably. Even with Mr Howard working longer days, the family were struggling to make ends meet. Things had become so dire that Sebastian's mother had reluctantly taken up a job minding toddlers in a day-care centre; an area in which there were lots of employment opportunities. This dismayed Sebastian no end, for it was the first time in his life that he found himself all alone in the house for hours at a time.

On the morning of the first day of her new job, Mrs Howard took off her necklace and handed it to her son. She told him that the pendant was very precious and that she didn't feel comfortable wearing it outside the house anymore. So she asked him to keep it somewhere safe. Sebastian put it in a hollow space beneath a loose floorboard in his bedroom that only he knew about. When he arrived home from school each day, he heated the dinner that his mother had left out for him in the microwave. Being all by himself in his family home was a strange feeling, and even after a few weeks he still hadn't gotten used to it. Mr or Mrs Howard would sometimes ring him on the house phone in the afternoons to make sure he was alright.

Sebastian and Adam's hatred of school had not abated, but they did manage to find some solace pursing their own scholarly interests during the evenings and at weekends. And on school day mornings they would occasionally bump into Mr Stevens when they debarked from the bus near the rehabilitation centre. For the former headmaster had been successful at his interview and was now a full-time employee at the centre. The boys gradually opened up to Mr Stevens and told him how much they hated the teachers at their new school and stories in their schoolbooks. It transpired that Mr Stevens was well aware of the *Moral Stories for Kids* books and agreed that they were dreadful.

More and more 'Wanted' posters were always appearing throughout the city streets. One afternoon after school, when the boys were walking towards the bus stop, Sebastian recognised a face in one of the photographs. It was Mr Maxwell. "That's the psychologist who diagnosed me with my mental problems," Sebastian told his friend as he pointed at Mr Maxwell's picture. The boys stood staring up at the poster and read through the accompanying information. It said that Mr Maxwell stood accused of bullying colleagues at the clinic where he worked by suggesting that they were incompetent (which had led to them making a formal complaint about him). His whereabouts were unknown, but the police urgently wanted to speak to him.

"How does suggesting your work colleagues are incompetent make you a bully?" Sebastian asked, scratching his head.

"I don't know..." Adam replied, feeling perplexed. "It's all a bit surreal," he added as the boys continued on their way.

* * *

One evening, Mr and Mrs Howard told Sebastian that the trial of the burglar who had broken into the Smiths' residence was scheduled to take place soon, and that the three of them would have to attend. They may be called to give evidence.

On the morning of the trial, Sebastian rose early and dressed in his best formal wear. He put on his little suit, a crisp white shirt and blue tie. Mr Howard drove his wife and son through the early morning traffic until they eventually arrived at the court building. They made their way inside and sat down in the public gallery. Sebastian began to grow apprehensive at the thought of testifying in a court of law. He looked around the courtroom. The walls were a dark cream colour and the paintwork was peeling in places. A musty smell hung in the air and sunlight seeped in through decorative windows.

The large wooden judge's bench stood imposingly at the front of room, and a plaque sitting atop the bench indicated that the magistrate trying today's case was Judge Charlie Johnson. On the wall just behind the bench there hung an old-fashioned portrait of a man sitting in a chair. He had white hair and a white, bushy beard, and one of his hands was tucked into his jacket. He reminded Sebastian of Santa Claus. Near the front of the court, Sebastian could see Adam and his parents chatting with their legal representatives. There didn't seem to be any sign of a jury anywhere, which struck Sebastian as strange; so he asked his father about this peculiarity.

"The jury system isn't used anymore. All cases are heard by the judge alone now," Mr Howard told him.

The air was filled with the sound of murmuring as people filed in, but everything went silent when the judge walked out from his quarters. He was pleasant-looking man with rosy cheeks and a big smile on his face. Beneath his judicial robe, Sebastian noticed that he wore jeans and trainers. As he was setting legal documents down on his bench, the burglar was led into courtroom flanked by two police officers. He wore the same clothes as the last time Sebastian saw him; a long black coat and black fedora hat. When he had taken his place in the dock, the judge turned towards him and began to speak.

"There are, alas, some formal legal procedures which we must follow here today. Do you understand?"

"Yes, Your Honour," the burglar replied.

Judge Charlie chuckled and informed the burglar that there was no need to call him 'Your Honour' or any other fancy title. His name was Charlie, and that's what he, the burglar, should call him. The thief smirked as the judge continued. "No one in this courtroom is any better or worse than you are. We are all equal here."

The burglar's smirk then broke into a grin, revealing his rotting teeth. "I can see that you're a good man, Charlie. Very compassionate and non-judgemental," he said.

"Thank you!" Judge Charlie responded, sitting up proudly in his chair. He then asked the defendant to state his name for the record.

"Pete Branden," the man replied.

After the breaking and entering and assault charges against him were read out, the judge asked Pete how he pled.

"Not guilty," Pete replied with a yawn. Then it was time for the Smiths to give their account of what had happened on the day of the alleged crime. One by one, Adam and his parents took to the witness box and described how Pete Branden had let himself into their house and then attacked Mr Smith. But as they spoke, Judge Charlie just kept looking at his watch and playing with his gavel. Mr Smith informed the judge that he had sustained several injuries during the attack, including flesh wounds and severe bruising. Judge Charlie asked Mr Smith if he had a medical report, but he said that he did not. In fact, he had not been medically examined yet as the doctor who was supposed to be attending to him was under investigation by the Medical Council for writing unwarranted prescriptions. Judge Charlie said that without a doctor's report he wouldn't entertain the claim that Mr Branden had injured Mr Smith.

When Adam and his parents had all finished providing testimony, it was the defendant's turn to speak. Judge Charlie invited Pete to tell the court about his life and what had led him to be in the Smiths' residence on the day of the alleged crime. The burglar gave a raspy cough and began. "I've been a drug addict since I was 12 years old and I'm always desperate for my next fix," he said. Judge Charlie asked him if he had made any serious attempt to get clean, but Pete replied that hadn't bothered as his doctor had told him that drug addiction is actually a disease. The judge nodded and Pete continued. "I never seem to have enough money to buy drugs so usually resort to thieving—"

"Sounds like you're a victim of poverty and inequality," Judge Charlie interjected.

There was silence for a few moments as Pete pondered over what the judge had just said. Then he looked out over the congregation in the courtroom and began to speak again. "Yes, that's right Charlie. If only we lived in a fairer, more egalitarian society, I wouldn't need to break into houses and steal from people," he pontificated, gesturing theatrically as he spoke.

The spectators in the gallery began to whisper amongst themselves. "Oh, he seems very intellectual," one of them said.

Pete went on to explain how he had let himself in through a window at Adam's family home and how Mr Smith had attacked him and restrained him for no reason. He added that the experience had left him suffering from post-traumatic stress disorder, and now even basic daily tasks such as collecting his welfare cheque were an ordeal. Judge Charlie listened credulously to everything Pete said.

"I'm terribly sorry to hear about how hard your life is Mr Branden," he murmured in a sympathetic tone, furrowing his brow.

Pete made a sad face and Judge Charlie continued. "I want to tell you Mr Branden, not just on my own behalf, not just on behalf of the judicial system, but literally on behalf of every single person in this country; we are extremely sorry for the way you have been treated by society. You are clearly the victim in this tragedy. Consider all charges against you dismissed!"

A broad smirk came across the burglar's drug-ridden, sunken cheeks, and he thrust his fist in the air in a triumphant gesture. When Judge Charlie wasn't looking, he stuck his tongue out at Adam's parents, causing Mrs Smith to burst into tears.

Judge Charlie rose to his feet and gave the burglar a thumbs-up. He then began to clap and urged everyone in the courtroom to join in. Gradually, members of the congregation stood up and started clapping for the burglar. Soon the sound of applause rang throughout the courtroom. But Sebastian and his parents were too shocked and dismayed to applaud. "Talk about the law being on the side of the criminal…" Mr Howard muttered.

As they were getting ready to leave, Sebastian noticed a movement in the aisle. He turned his head and saw a member of the court's staff walking in his direction with his eyes fixed directly on him. The man leaned down. "Come on little boy, don't be the odd one out. Mr Branden has low self-esteem and we all need to help make him feel good about himself." Against his better judgement, Sebastian began to clap.

As Pete stood down from the dock, members of his legal team rushed over and shook his hand. But Sebastian was frustrated. Neither he nor his parents had been called upon to testify, and he felt that the judge had been ridiculously lenient on the burglar. As Judge Charlie was walking back towards his chambers, Sebastian stood up from his seat and began waving over at him.

"Your Honour, I witnessed everything that happened at Adam's house!" he shouted. But the judge just ignored him. Sebastian's parents told their son to quieten down, as it wasn't acceptable to shout at a judge like that. However, Sebastian was too annoyed to pay any heed. Just before the judge left the courtroom he yelled out, "The burglar didn't break into Adam's house because he's a victim! He did it because he's a self-centred thug!"

The court immediately went silent. All eyes were on Sebastian. Pete glared at him, while Judge Charlie stood frozen with his mouth agape. Then his facial expression hardened.

"What did you say!?" he bellowed.

Sebastian was about to recount to the court his recollection of the break-in, but a member of the Smiths' legal team interposed. "Young Sebastian has recently been diagnosed with some mental issues," he said.

There was murmuring in the court as people began to chatter amongst themselves in hushed tones.

"The poor little chap!" the judge said. "Don't worry, there's hope for you yet young man," he added, giving Sebastian a wink. Judge Charlie then looked over at the court stenographer and told her to scratch everything Sebastian had said from the record.

Later that evening, back at their home, Sebastian and his parents ate dinner and watched television. When there was a knock at the front door, Mrs Howard answered. It was the Smiths. They had come to thank their friends for the moral support they provided throughout their ordeal with the burglar and his ensuing trial. In particular, they thanked Sebastian for his courage in the courtroom, and said it was unfortunate that the judge hadn't given him the opportunity to speak.

Mr Smith said that after everything they had been through, they were considering emigrating to the United States (the Smiths all held American citizenship as both Adam and his father had been born there). The Howards were saddened at the thought of their friends potentially moving away, but the Mr Smith emphasised that nothing had been decided for certain yet. The two families chatted late into the evening, consuming many cups of tea. Eventually, the Smiths said they had better get back home as they were tired from the stressful day. Just as they were standing up to leave, a newsflash suddenly appeared on the television. The newscaster announced that from tomorrow onwards, all domestic electricity and gas heating in the country would be turned off at 8.00p.m. each night in an effort to curb global warming. They would be turned back on 12 hours later, at 8.00a.m. Everybody groaned loudly.

"Whatever next?" Mrs Howard asked rhetorically, wondering whether or not this would be a short-term measure.

* * *

The next morning at school, everyone was talking about the fact that the electricity and gas would be switched off at night. Ms Joyce said that all the children should be very proud that they were playing their part in preventing climate change from destroying the planet, and advised them to remind their parents to boil the kettles for hot-water-bottles before eight o'clock.

In light of the government's latest policy, Ms Joyce started the morning with a science lesson about global warming. "Scientists have proved that the world keeps getting hotter and hotter because of all the gases that go up into the atmosphere from factories, machines, cars and so on..." Sebastian sat attentively throughout the lesson, happy to be learning some new information. He was curious about whether there was any disagreement in the scientific community about the cause of global warming, but knew there was no point in asking Ms Joyce. The school day progressed as normal, and when break-time eventually came, all the children made their way to the canteen.

Adam took a chess set out of his bag and asked his friends if either of them fancied a game. But David said he'd rather a game of football. In fact, he'd brought a football with him to school – a little green one. He suggested that they gather a group of children together and sneak across the road to the sports pitches to play a match.

Neither Sebastian nor Adam was too enthused by the idea, but David was unrelenting. He asked them to go find Tyrone, as he was good at football apparently. Sebastian replied that he wasn't sure it was a good idea for Tyrone to play with them, considering he was usually so hot-headed. But David commented that he was actually alright once you got to know him. So, as David walked around the canteen asking boys if they wanted to play a football match, Adam and Sebastian went and searched for Tyrone. After looking for 10 minutes they still hadn't located him, and so the assembled group of amateur footballers headed off for the pitch without him. David led the way. When Mr Redmond wasn't looking, David pushed open the school gate and everybody slowly crept out. Sebastian felt a little guilty about breaking the school rules, but also a sense of exhilaration. They waited until there was a gap in the traffic to cross the main road, and headed to the nearby sports ground. David divided the children into two teams. Knowing that Sebastian and Adam weren't exactly sporty types, he decided that they should both be goalkeepers. So Adam joined David's team, and Sebastian joined the opposing team.

Within a few minutes, the play was underway. The match hadn't progressed very far when Tyrone suddenly appeared.

"Why didn't you guys tell me you were playing football!? Was you trying to exclude me?!" he asked angrily.

Sebastian hurried over to him and explained that himself and Adam had in fact looked for him, but couldn't find him anywhere. Tyrone just huffed and ran onto the pitch. David asked him to join his team and the match resumed. Sebastian was spending a lot of time just idly standing by the goal posts as the rest of the boys kicked the football around. Feeling a bit peckish, he reached into his trouser pocket and pulled out a banana he had brought from home. As he was nibbling on it, Tyrone screamed piercingly, "Kick It Out!"

Sebastian looked around and saw that the football had landed a few feet away from him. He ran over and quickly booted it back onto the field.

Tyrone played in a very aggressive fashion and kept violently tackling the other players. Eventually, he began bounding towards Sebastian, kicking the ball ahead of him. He struck it with all his might and it flew high into the air. Sebastian became flustered as he tried to position himself along the trajectory of the speeding ball. He stretched his hands out and closed his eyes. The football fell straight into his arms. Tyrone was livid and began cursing. Sebastian quickly kicked the ball back onto the pitch. The boys continued to play for another half an hour, with Sebastian managing to save every attempt on his goal.

"*I'm actually pretty good at this*," he thought to himself. Things weren't going quite so well for Adam though, and he conceded four goals. Towards the end of the game, Sebastian could see that Tyrone was furious. As a token gesture, he allowed him to score.

"Hurray!" Tyrone cheered, and ran around the pitch dancing.

Shortly after, the boys heard the distant sound of Mr Redmond ringing the school bell. Lunchtime was over, so they made their way back across the main road to the school playground. They slunk down low, and tiptoed back in through the school gate. As everyone was heading back to class, Sebastian stopped to use the lavatory. When he was done, he continued along the school corridor and suddenly heard a voice behind him.

"Toff!" the voice shouted.

Sebastian spun around. There, standing in the middle of the corridor was Nick, the school bully. Even with his eyes crossed, Sebastian could tell that he was looking at him.

He tried to run, but Nick stomped forward, grabbed him by the shoulders and threw him to the ground. The bully began slapping him about the head. Sebastian tried to shove him away, but this only made Nick increase the severity of his slaps.

"Somebody help me!" Sebastian shouted at the top of his voice as he tried to push to bully away.

Hearing his shouts, one of the school's teachers, Mr Hays, rushed out of his classroom. He ran over and broke up the scuffle. "This behaviour is totally unacceptable," he kept repeating. Mr Hays brought Sebastian and Nick to the staffroom and began to interview the boys about what had happened. He asked Nick to tell his side of the story first.

"I thought I'd teach that kid a lesson," Nick began. "I'm always seeing him and his two mates waltzing around the school, acting like they own the place or somethin'. They're all airs and graces and stuff."

"Is that true?" Mr Hays asked, looking to Sebastian.

"My friends and I don't act like we own the school!" Sebastian protested. "I was just walking down the corridor when Nick called me a toff and started beating me up. I called out for help and tried to push him off of me."

"I've heard enough…" Mr Hays said. "You're as bad as each other."

Sebastian once more tried to explain that Nick was in the wrong for assaulting him, and that he, Sebastian, did the right thing by trying to defend himself and calling for help. But Mr Hays just exhaled and again said that the two boys were equally as bad as each other. Sebastian was astonished by the teacher's apparent inability to make even the most basic distinction between right and wrong. All the while, Nick stood silently with his eyes fixed on Sebastian, continuously giving him an intimidating stare. Mr Hays asked the boys their names and then wrote out notes for their parents.

As Sebastian walked back to class, he opened the note to see what Mr Hays had written. "*Dear Mr and Mrs Howard. This note is to inform you that Sebastian and another boy (Nick) got into a brawl today at school. I am satisfied that Sebastian played his part in initiating the fight and gave as much as he got. Signed, Jack Hays, Form Teacher.*"

Sebastian began to feel upset, mainly because he'd been assaulted, but also because of the wording of the note.

However, he knew that his parents would listen to his version of events and would see sense.

And indeed, later that evening after he had explained the situation to them, Mr Howard told his son not to worry about the note. He said he wouldn't take too seriously anything the teachers at Sebastian's school said as they all seemed like a bunch of fruitcakes. However, he urged Sebastian to stay out of Nick's orbit from now on, as it seemed that he couldn't rely on his teachers to protect him from the bully.

As eight o'clock approached, Sebastian sat on his bed and kept staring out his bedroom window. Shortly before the impeding moment, Mr and Mrs Howard joined their son in his bedroom and Mrs Howard put a hot-water-bottle in the bed to warm it up. The three family members then stared out the window intently, and sure enough, at eight o'clock exactly, each and every light in the city began to flicker. Then they all extinguished and darkness prevailed. But within seconds, twinkling stars appeared in the clear night sky and the faint glow of candlelight dotted the cityscape. Mr Howard went around all the rooms in the house lighting candles.

Sebastian got into bed and pulled the duvet up over him. Mrs Howard tucked him in. "It's going to be cold tonight Sebastian," she said softly, noting that it would be 12 hours before they had electrical power and heating again.

"They have electricity," Sebastian said, sitting up and looking out the window.

"Who?" she asked. "The people in that big house over there," he replied, pointing to a building far off in the distance, which was shining brightly in the otherwise dim city.

"Hmm, that's the rehabilitation centre," Mrs Howard replied. "It must have its own generator."

Minutes later, Sebastian's father came back into the room and pulled down the blinds. The couple wished their son a goodnight and closed his bedroom door as they left.

"We'll have to listen out for any strange noises during the night," Sebastian overheard his father tell his mother as they walked off towards their own bedroom. "Without electricity the alarm system doesn't work, and we have little protection from intruders..."

Sebastian shuddered.

He lay down and tried to get to sleep, but for a full hour the thought of an intruder breaking in kept playing on his mind. Also, his bedroom was so cold that he could see his breath in the night air. So he slunk down under the duvet and curled up into a foetal position. Eventually, he nodded off.

* * *

In class the next morning, Ms Joyce began asking everyone how they had coped last night without any electricity. Sebastian remarked that he spent most of the night shivering because of the cold, and Adam and David commented that they had had similar experiences.

"Now you know how poor people feel," the teacher replied sarcastically.

The boys didn't respond to the comment, and just took their seats. As the day went on, Sebastian began to develop the snivels, then a sore throat and headache. He tried to keep his head down and avoid eye contact with his teacher, but sensing that he was trying to evade her attention, Ms Joyce kept asking him to read moral stories out to the class.

By the time he arrived back at his house that afternoon, Sebastian felt terrible. He immediately went to his bedroom, closed the blinds and lay down on his bed. When his mother came in from work he told her that he thought he had the flu. Mrs Howard went to the kitchen and grabbed a thermometer from the medicine cabinet.

"You're burning up!" she said as she took Sebastian's temperature. She told him that he should have an early night; hopefully he might feel better by the morning.

Mrs Howard made Sebastian a hot-water-bottle and tucked him into bed. When Mr Howard arrived through the front door that evening, he went straight into the living room where his wife was watching a movie on television. "Sebastian's not feeling too well," she told him.

"I hope it's nothing too serious," he replied, "The last thing we need now is for one of us to fall ill – we have enough problems as it is."

After having a cup of tea and reading the evening newspapers, Mr Howard climbed the stairs and opened his son's bedroom door. But by now Sebastian was fast asleep and snoring lightly.

* * *

Early the next morning, the Howards asked their son how he was feeling.

"Horrible... I have aches and pains all over, and I feel sick."

Mrs Howard put her hand on his forehead. "Your temperature is still very high. I'll ring your school to let them know you won't be in today, and then ask our doctor to see if he can make a house call," she said.

She went back downstairs and Sebastian could hear her talking on the telephone. A few minutes later she returned and told him that she had rang his school and informed them that he wouldn't be in today due to illness. But unfortunately, it turned out that their family doctor had emigrated.

"I think you'll just have to ride this one out," she said, looking at her son with a sad expression.

Mrs Howard refreshed Sebastian's hot-water-bottle and placed a plastic basin beside his bed – just in case. She said she would take the day off work so that she could stay home and nurse him. Sebastian's father said he'd better get a move on so as not to be late for work.

"I hope you feel better soon," he told his son as he left.

Sebastian slept on and off throughout most of the day. But during the late afternoon he woke up feeling worse than ever. He was nauseous, his nose was blocked, and his head was pounding. Just when he thought things couldn't get any worse, the doorbell rang. He heard the front door open and then the sound of voices. Seconds later a troupe of footsteps began making their way up the stairs.

"Look who's here to see you," Sebastian's mother said as she opened his bedroom door. It was Ms Joyce and a group of five children from class; three boys and two girls. Although Sebastian knew the children to see, he had never spoken to them before.

Mrs Howard leaned down close to her son and pretended to fix his pillow. "I'm sorry Sebastian. I didn't want to let them in but Ms Joyce was very insistent," she whispered. Ms

Joyce quickly interrupted. "We've come to visit you so you don't feel excluded," she stated in her usual monotone.

Sebastian told his teacher that he felt dreadful and would rather just be left alone, but Ms Joyce paid no notice. "Don't worry. I have something that will make you feel better," she said as she pulled a small packet of green powder out of her purse. "It's a herbal remedy. Tribes in the Amazon rainforest use this to treat ailments," she said. She then poured the powder into a glass of water sitting on the bedside cabinet and handed it to him. "No, please, I don't want it," Sebastian said, trying to push it away.

But Ms Joyce just kept thrusting the concoction into Sebastian's face until he finally agreed to drink it, just to keep her quiet.

"It tastes horrible," he sighed.

Some of the children began looking around the bedroom and started playing with Sebastian's toys. One of the boys kept looking up at the poster of the solar system that David had bought Sebastian for his birthday. He then stood up on his tiptoes and tore it off the wall.

"Oh look! There's a football with a treasure map on it!" a girl said, pointing to a globe sitting on top of Sebastian's bookcase. She started to climb up the bookshelf to reach the object, and just as she was nearing the top, the whole shelf collapsed. Books scattered all over the carpet and the globe landed on the floor with an almighty crash. Ms Joyce was stunned.

"My goodness, this house is a death-trap!" she exclaimed.

"Please stop. You're destroying my bedroom," Sebastian groaned as Mrs Howard rushed about trying to control the children.

Sebastian could feel his heart racing and noticed that everything in the room looked like it was spinning.

"I think I'm dying" he whispered.

"Quick, drink more of the herbal remedy," Ms Joyce said. Aware that the teacher was under the impression that Sebastian still took pills for his mental problems, Mrs Howard suggested that the remedy might be interacting with the medication.

"That's a good point, I never thought of that," Ms Joyce replied, placing the glass back down on the bedside cabinet.

Sebastian's mother said it would be best for her son to get some rest now, but the teacher ignored her. She took a copy of *Moral Stories for Kids* out of her handbag and began reading *Homeless Harry* to Sebastian.

On wet and windy nights, Harry would sleep in a doorway with only a tinfoil hat to keep him sheltered from the rain. One evening, a kindly man named Mr Jones came over to Harry and asked him if he was alright. A look of horror appeared on Harry's face.

"You're out to get me, aren't you?! Everybody is out to get me!" he said.

"I'm not out to get you," Mr Jones replied reassuringly.

Mr Jones took Harry by the hand and led him back to his apartment. He introduced him to his partner and kids and let him sleep in the spare room. In time, Harry became a cherished member of the Jones' household. He was a wonderful storyteller, and kept everyone entertained for hours on end with his farfetched yarns about aliens and UFOs.

After the reading, Ms Joyce produced her video camera and began aiming it at Sebastian. But Mrs Howard was beginning to lose her patience. "I'd rather you didn't record my son. This is my house, so my rules," she said firmly. Ms Joyce seemed irked, but relented and put the camera back into her bag. However, she kept asking Sebastian if he had understood the moral of the story. Feeling too unwell to argue with her, Sebastian quickly blurted out what he knew Ms Joyce wanted to hear.

"We should all make more of an effort to include homeless people in our lives…" With that, Sebastian's stomach started to spasm and he leaned over the basin that his mother had left beside his bed and began to retch.

Mrs Howard patted him on the back, and when he was finished he lay back down in his bed and closed his eyes. "I really think Sebastian needs to rest now," Mrs Howard said. "Anyway it's getting late. My husband will be home from work soon and I need to make him his dinner."

Ms Joyce suggested that she and the children join the family for their meal. But Sebastian's mother didn't reply. She just led them all back down the stairs and showed them to the door. When the uninvited guests had left, Mrs Howard made her way back up to her son's bedroom. But Sebastian had fallen asleep, and so she quietly closed the door over to let him rest.

A couple of hours later, Sebastian woke up feeling a little bit better. His temperature had come down and his headache had subsided slightly. However, he was certain that the improvement was due to the bug running its course rather than a result of Ms Joyce's quasi-medical intervention. He felt a bit hungry so his mother made him a few slices of toast. A little while later, the doorbell rang again. Sebastian froze in horror. But thankfully it was just Adam and David who had come to see how their friend was feeling.

Sebastian told his mother that he was feeling well enough to entertain them, and so she showed the boys to his room. Sebastian informed them that Ms Joyce and some children from their class had paid him a visit, but it turned out that they already knew.

"She said that she was coming to visit you, and asked if anyone would like to accompany her." Adam said.

“Naturally, we asked if we could tag along” David interjected, taking over the story. “But she told us that we spend enough time with you as it is, and said she wanted some of the other kids in our class to get know you better.”

“Well, I’m very annoyed at her,” Sebastian said, and clued the boys in about what had happened. Although Adam and David were well used to their teacher’s arrogance, they were still taken aback that she would come into Sebastian’s home and behave as she did. The boys continued chatting for a few minutes and when Sebastian asked how their school day had been, Adam and David told him that there had been a big incident. Nick the bully had called Tyrone and Naomi rude names and shouted insults at them. The school had finally decided to expel him. The police had even been called and had taken him away in handcuffs.

“About time!” Sebastian declared.

CHAPTER 8

By Christmas (or the 'Winter Holiday' as it was now officially known), Sebastian's flu had cleared and he was back to good health. Usually at that time of year, the city was awash with Christmas trees, holly wreaths, flashing lights, plastic Santa Clauses and reindeer. However, the government had introduced a new rule that forbade Christmas decorations in case they caused offence to religious minority groups. Thus, it was the first Christmas in living memory that the city was devoid of any such decorations.

Nonetheless, the Smiths and Howards illicitly put up some festive decorations inside their homes, well away from the prying eyes of the police and government bureaucrats. The two families had a quiet Winter Holiday, not least because of treacherous weather conditions. However, an abundance of snow did inevitably lead to numerous snowball fights between Sebastian and Adam, as well as the building of several snowmen. In the evenings, the two families would sit in front of the open fire in the Howards living room, eat mince pies, cakes and sweets, and sing Christmas carols (all expenses were paid by the Smith family, as a kind gesture of friendship).

As a new year dawned, all residents on the street received an important letter from the local council that stated that, at over 100 years old, their houses were deemed a safety risk and would thus be demolished. However, the letter added that the residents would be moved into lovely, new, state-of-the-art apartments. It was clear to Sebastian that his parents were distraught at the news.

"Life in this country has become intolerable," Mr Howard kept saying.

The Smiths called round to the Howards' house to discuss the letter. That evening was a stormy one, and after they had hung their wet coats in the hall, they joined the Howard family in the living room, in front of the open fire. They said that they had considered challenging the council's decision to demolish the houses, but then realised that they would be wasting their time. The council wouldn't care what they had to say and would just demolish them anyhow. To make matters worse for the Smiths, their solicitor had told them that Pete Branden and his legal team were preparing a case against Mr Smith for assault and false imprisonment.

"We have decided to emigrate to New York," Mr Smith said, adjusting his gold cufflinks as he spoke. "We will be leaving in a few weeks."

"Would you consider coming with us?" Mrs Smith asked the Howards, fidgeting with her pearl necklace.

Sebastian loved the idea, for he was becoming increasingly disenchanted with how things were getting worse and worse all around him. "Yes!" he blurted out before his parents even had a chance to answer. "We could all go and live in America together!" he squealed in delight, hopping about the living room with excitement.

"This country's bankrupt," Mr Smith continued. "Rumour has it that the government will soon begin seizing people's bank accounts. So if you do decide to leave, you might want to do it sooner rather than later."

"Goodness!" Sebastian's parents said in shock. "Yes, yes, in that case I think we might have to seriously consider our options," Mrs Howard replied, putting her fingers to the bridge of her nose.

"We'll look into it," Mr Howard said, putting his arm around his wife.

When the Smiths had left, the Howards explained to Sebastian that thousands of people around the world were desperately trying to move to America, but that only a tiny proportion of them were allowed in. Hence, even if they applied for visas, the chance of their application being successful was very slight. They told Sebastian not to get his hopes up, and to just assume that they would be staying put for the foreseeable future.

* * *

As it turned out, Adam only sat through another fortnight of school before the Smiths left. When he told everyone that he was to leave, David was upset while Ms Joyce seemed indifferent. Sebastian and Adam spent almost every moment during that two-week period together. They watched movies, played board games, and went for walks in the local park. As the inevitable approached, they cleared out the tree house and Sebastian helped Adam pack his belongings.

Mr and Mrs Howard set their alarm clock for very early on the chilly Saturday morning of their friends' departure, so they could see them off. The first thing Sebastian did when he awoke was to lean up against the corner of his bedroom window and look up the street. Through the frost-covered glass he could see a removal van parked outside Adam's house. Workmen were busy loading the last of the family's belongings inside, to be sent along to them shortly after they arrived in America. (Most of their possessions had already been shipped, although Mr Smith was still trying to organise the transportation of his racehorses.) Sebastian got dressed and quickly ran down the stairs. He walked with his parents the few paces down the street to the Smiths' house.

They met the Smith family as they were coming out of their front door. While the adults chatted, Sebastian and Adam embraced. The boys were well aware that it might be a long time before they saw each other again, and their eyes welled up with tears as they bid each other farewell. Mrs Smith reminded them that they could talk to each other on the phone from time to time, which helped alleviate their moroseness slightly. Soon, a taxi pulled up on the kerb and Adam and his parents climbed in. They waved goodbye to the Howards as the car left for the airport.

Days after their departure, the newspapers reported that the government was, just as Mr Smith had predicted, trying to rush through legislation which would allow it to seize people's bank accounts. For Sale signs sprung up all over the city as more and more people moved abroad, but with the failing economy, few houses sold. Moreover, the extravagant rights which the government had afforded tenants dissuaded the houses owners from letting them. Consequently, many lay empty and had begun to fall into disrepair. Broken windows and graffiti were now a common sight.

* * *

For most of the week after his best friend's departure, Sebastian felt sorrowful. His parents applied for visas for America but had not yet heard as to the outcome of the application. However, Sebastian's mood was to change for the better on Friday afternoon, when he returned home from school and noticed that a letter had come, addressed to him. This was quite unusual because, as a 10 year-old boy, Sebastian didn't normally get any post. He quickly tore open the white envelope and pulled out the letter inside. It was from the judges of the international essay writing competition that he had entered months previously. They wished to thank him for entering the competition and were pleased to inform him that his essay on the topic of the abolition of the slave trade had won first prize! Fastened to the top of the letter with a paperclip was a cheque for €250. Sebastian felt ecstatic and jumped for joy. The first thing he thought to do was run round to the Smiths' house and tell Adam the good news, but then he remembered that the Smiths had emigrated.

Sebastian kept reading the letter over and over and counted down the hours until his parents came home from work. When they eventually arrived, they were thrilled for their son. Each gave him a big hug and told him how proud they were of him. Sebastian said that he wanted to take them out for a nice meal to celebrate. So they changed into formal wear and set off for one of their favourite restaurants. They hadn't been there for a long time as the family couldn't afford to eat out much anymore. When they arrived, they noticed that the restaurant had changed considerably since their last visit. It was decorated with modern art, the service was dreadful, and the food tasted disgusting. The Howards were a bit disappointed, although they had come to expect a poor standard from most businesses operating in the city. As they finished up and paid for their meal, they decided not to leave a tip. The young waitress made a sarcastic comment as they left, but they pretended not to hear.

* * *

The Smiths rang over the weekend. They were living temporarily with Mr Smith's parents in New York City, until they bought themselves a new house. Mr and Mrs Smith chatted to the Howards for a little while, and then let the boys speak to each other.

"It's amazing here, Sebastian," Adam said. "Everyone rushes around, but you don't have to be afraid of what you say all the time." Adam spoke with such excitement that Sebastian could barely get a word in edgeways. "And the skyscrapers in the city are enormous! We'll be taking a trip up the Empire State Building tomorrow." The boys chatted for a further 10 minutes and Adam was delighted for Sebastian when he informed him about winning the essay competition. "You're so smart!" he said.

* * *

On Monday morning, Sebastian alighted from the bus outside the rehabilitation centre as usual. He paced back and forth by the front steps of the centre, eagerly waiting for Mr Stevens to arrive for work. But after 10 minutes there was still no sign of him, and so he decided to continue on to school. "*He must have gone in already*," he thought. He made his way to his classroom, which was gradually filling up with children. As usual, Ms Joyce was at her desk completing some paperwork.

"You look like you had a good weekend," she said when she saw Sebastian grinning.

"Yes, I won first place in an international essay writing competition!" he told her.

"Is that right?" the teacher replied dismissively.

Without giving Sebastian a chance to elaborate, Ms Joyce began asking all the other children in the class what they had done over the weekend.

"I, like, made this collage of my favourite boy band," Chantelle said, holding up a sheet of paper with some pictures glued onto it. "It's wicked, isn't it?"

"Oh my goodness!" said Ms Joyce, becoming quite animated. "Look at this! Wow! Everybody look at what Chantelle made!" The other children in the room directed their gaze towards Chantelle's collage and began to holler. The teacher pointed to a picture of one of boy band members and, in a rare attempt at humour, said, "Oh yeah! Look at the six-pack on him!"

Chantelle sniggered.

As Ms Joyce continued to chat to Chantelle, David arrived into class. Sebastian rushed over and told him about his award and showed him the letter from the judges. David congratulated Sebastian and gave him a pat on the back. As he began to read through the letter, Ms Joyce suddenly marched over and looked at Sebastian with dagger eyes, clearly annoyed.

"Yes, you were very lucky to win that competition, Sebastian. There's no need to keep boasting about it!" Sebastian informed her that he had worked strenuously for weeks on end writing the essay, and in the letter the judges noted that it was one of the best essays they had ever read. Ms Joyce rolled her eyes and exhaled. She explained that the judges in such competitions actually select the winner at random, and therefore he was just lucky. "Put the letter away now," she told him sternly.

Sebastian grudgingly did as he was asked.

The teacher continued asking the children in the class to tell her what they had done over the weekend. Tyrone said that he had written a rap song. This made Ms Joyce very excited and she asked him to perform it for the class. Tyrone stood up and immediately burst into a rap, rapidly speaking dozens of words in quick succession. "*Me want to make me riches while me dancin' with me bit#hes...*" As he performed, his twin sister Naomi started making beat-box sounds, Chantelle did a robotic dance and Austin started to rock back and forth.

"It's good!" Ms Joyce said.

"It's good" Austin replied.

But Sebastian was appalled by the rap's vile misogynistic lyrics and covered his ears. In contrast, David could appreciate the talent in the rhyming words.

"You need to be more open-minded Sebastian," he said. "Rap isn't better or worse than any other form of musical expression, just different."

When Tyrone was finished, everyone applauded. Noticing that Sebastian had his hands held up to his ears for most of the performance, Ms Joyce asked him what type of music he liked. He deliberated for a moment about whether he should answer honestly, but confessed that he liked Beethoven and Chopin. The classroom erupted into fits of laughter. Even Ms Joyce joined in and wiped a tear away from her eye.

"Sebastian thinks he's better than everyone else!" someone shouted.

"What are Baythopen and Chovan?" another child asked, confused.

Sebastian blushed and put his head down.

Prompted by Chantelle's lovely collage, Ms Joyce decided that they would have a collage-making art exercise. She gathered up a bundle of magazines from the staffroom and distributed them among her class. But she soon realised that they were running low on glue so she asked Sebastian to go to the caretaker's office to get some.

As he walked down the corridor, he heard shuffling noises coming from the school bursary. As he got closer, he could hear voices whispering. The bursary door was slightly ajar and he peeked in. Although the room was in darkness, there were flashes of torchlight. Mystified, Sebastian pushed the door wide open. Light flooded in revealing three teachers, Mr Hays, Ms Jackson, and Ms Mills creeping about. Wads of cash were sticking out from Mr Hays' bulging pockets and from the women's handbags. They all turned towards the door, looking shaken.

"The light isn't working," Mr Hays uttered when he saw Sebastian.

Sebastian tried the switch on the wall and the room instantly lit up.

"Oh, it's working again!" Ms Mills said jubilantly.

"We're just, umm, transferring the bursary funds to another room," Ms Jackson blurted out, talking over her colleagues. The teachers then told Sebastian to go about his business and quickly pulled the door shut, so he continued on to the caretaker's office and obtained a bottle of glue from Mr McHugh.

Back in the class, Ms Joyce was organising children into little groups of three or four. Sebastian gave her the glue, and she told him to sit with a group of three other children; two girls and a boy (none of whom he knew very well).

"What should we make a collage of?" one of the girls asked, looking at Sebastian expectantly.

Rather than risk angering them by suggesting a topic considered too cultured, he suggested a collage featuring modes of transport: cars, airplanes, buses, etc. The children agreed and they all got to work. Ms Joyce helped her students cut out pictures from the magazines and place them on sheets of A3 paper. Sebastian felt apathetic and looked around at the group in which David was working. Their project was a medley of football players.

After about half an hour, Ms Joyce walked around the classroom eyeing all the colourful collages. "Which one is the best?" David asked her.

Everyone went quiet, wondering which collage their teacher would deem her favourite. "They're all the best!" she declared ecstatically, and went around sticking a little gold star onto the top corner of each one. The room erupted into screams of delight, and several students began to cry tears of happiness.

But soon it was time to get back to work. Ms Joyce taught geography, followed by some moral stories, and then history.

When lunchtime eventually arrived, Sebastian stood idly by the schoolyard railings watching traffic speed by. He heard someone calling his name and followed the voice over to some rubbish bins by the playground's perimeter. Hiding behind them was David and Greg, smoking cigarettes. Danny the squirrel leapt about on his master's shoulders, trying to evade the wisps of white smoke.

"Fancy a drag?" David asked. Sebastian replied that he did not, and informed the two boys that smoking is bad for one's health.

Suddenly, Danny leapt from Greg's shoulder and scurried out through the school gate. Greg dropped his cigarette and rushed after the ginger rodent. He pulled open the gate and darted across the road to a little copse of trees and weeds on the other side. He crawled around on his hands and knees looking for his pet as Sebastian and David looked on from the playground. Eventually Greg located the animal and perched him back on his shoulder. As he was about to cross back over the road, he reached into his trouser pocket and pulled out a cigarette and a lighter. Just as he was lighting up, a black car came speeding around the corner. The couple inside appeared to be arguing and weren't paying attention to the road.

"Greg! Watch out!" Sebastian screamed. But it was too late. The car ploughed into Greg with a loud thud and then screeched to a stop.

Sebastian and David rushed out through the gate and over to their stricken schoolmate. He was writhing in agony on the ground and his leg was bent at an awkward angle. Danny the squirrel was in an even worse state. He had been crushed under the car's wheels and his flattened body lay stuck to the tarmac road. The driver and his wife jumped out of the car and rushed over to the boys. They looked traumatised as they gazed down at the injured Greg.

"Oh dear, this isn't good!" the man said.

Sebastian waved over to Mr Redmond who was pacing back and forth across the playground, talking to himself. He rushed over, followed by a group of children.

"That man knocked Greg down," David said, pointing at the car's driver who stood there in a daze.

"No, no, my wife was driving, not me," he replied. His wife gave him a filthy look.

"Well, we'd better call for an ambulance," Mr Redmond said as he took his mobile phone out of his pocket. He then began to usher all the children back towards the school.

Back in the classroom, David told Ms Joyce about what had happened to Greg. She was very distressed by the news, but told everybody to sit down as they needed to get back to work. The class were only about five minutes into the day's maths lesson when Mr Wallace burst in carrying a folder in his arms. He stood with Ms Joyce at the front of the class and chatted about the accident with Greg. There was a slight hush in the room as the children tried to listen to what the two adults were saying. Mr Wallace told Ms Joyce that he had determined that she was the last teacher to arrive at the school that morning, and that she hadn't locked the gate after her. Ms Joyce replied that she was fairly certain that she had in fact locked the gate.

But the head teacher produced a sheet of paper from his folder and handed it to her. "You ticked the box indicating that you closed the gate after you, but didn't lock it," he said pointing at the sheet. Ms Joyce put her hand up to her forehead and moaned.

"Maybe I ticked the wrong box," she said, adding that all the box-ticking could get confusing sometimes.

Mr Wallace frowned and asked her if she could prove to him that she had locked the gate after she had come in. The teacher stared ahead blankly for a few moments.

"No," she replied.

Mr Wallace told her to be more careful in future, and then left, slamming the door after him. Ms Joyce seemed peeved, but nevertheless continued with her teaching duties. At the end of the school day Sebastian noticed how dejected she looked as she packed her belongings into her handbag. He felt sorry for her.

* * *

The next morning at school, Ms Joyce introduced a new pupil to the class. "This is Stefan," she said, placing her hands on the shoulders of a little boy standing beside her at the front of the room. Stefan was a roguish-looking boy, wearing a brown jumper and baggy trousers. He smiled and gave a big wave to his new classmates. Ms Joyce leaned down to him. "Could you tell us something about yourself?" she asked, speaking very slowly. Stefan looked up at the teacher.

"*Familia mea și m-am mutat în această țară pentru a profita de sistemul de protecție socială,*" he replied.

Nobody had the faintest idea what he had just said.

"Okay, that's great!" Ms Joyce exclaimed and then turned back to the class. "Stefan recently moved here from overseas and doesn't speak much English. So we are going to spend an hour each morning helping him learn the language." She pointed to a free seat beside Sebastian (where Adam used to sit), and Stefan sat down. Ms Joyce then instructed the new student on how to introduce himself in English, writing "Hello, my name is Stefan" on the whiteboard. Stefan read the sentence aloud and then started to write it in his copybook.

Sebastian grumbled to himself, but he said nothing, lest he incur the wrath of his classmates.

Glancing over at what Stefan was writing, Sebastian noticed that he was spelling some of the words incorrectly. So he took the initiative to help him with the exercise. He reached over and pointed out to Stefan his mistakes, and showed him how each word should be spelt. But Ms Joyce quickly rushed over and asked Sebastian what he was doing. When he explained that he was helping Stefan with the spellings, Ms Joyce crossed her arms and looked displeased.

"There's no right or wrong way to spell," she said, "only different ways." As Sebastian had long given up trying to reason with his teacher, he said nothing and turned back to his own desk.

Feeling bored and frustrated as Ms Joyce continued the lesson, he went to look at his watch, but much to his surprise he wasn't wearing it. He looked around his desk and on the floor, but couldn't see it anywhere. Sebastian tried to communicate to Stefan that he had lost his watch by pointing at his wrist, but Stefan just stared at him with a big Cheshire cat grin. Just as he began to wonder whether he had actually put it on that morning, there was a knock on the classroom door.

"Could I have a word with you please Ms Joyce?" Mr Wallace asked as he walked in. "It's urgent." The head teacher led Ms Joyce to the staffroom where all the teachers and the school's bursar, Mr Darlington, had hurriedly gathered for an impromptu meeting. So important was the reason for the meeting that the teachers were prepared to leave their students unsupervised for a little while. Ms Joyce had a seat and everyone crowded around her. Mr Wallace informed her that someone had been stealing from the school bursary, and they suspected it was her. As everyone leered at Ms Joyce, he asked if she could prove that she hadn't stolen any money.

"No, I can't" Ms Joyce said, and began to weep.

"In that case, I have no choice but to fire you," Mr Wallace stated emphatically. But without warning, Ms Joyce stood up from her seat and a look of fury formed on her face. "I'm tired of being blamed every time something goes wrong in this school!" she snapped. "In fact, I have already contacted my union representative and he's coming here to talk to you today! Here he is now actually," she said, pointing out the window at a red sports car pulling in through the school gate. And so, Ms Joyce and her union representative squabbled with Mr Wallace and the other teachers long into the afternoon. But all the while, back in the teacherless classrooms, things were descending into anarchy.

Children were drawing on their desks and throwing their schoolbooks around. Tyrone dashed about menacingly, pretending to shoot everybody with his outstretched finger, while Chantelle and Naomi starting arguing and pulling each other's hair. "You're minging!" Chantelle kept yelling. All the noise was becoming too much for Austin and he started to have a tantrum. He lay down on the floor and began banging his head against the ground. Slowly but surely, students made their way out into the school's corridors, pulling paintings from the walls and smashing windows as they went. In the assembly hall they threw chairs about and when they arrived down in the canteen, they helped themselves to drinks and snacks.

Eventually, the children decided to escape the confines of their school. A few of the bigger students began ramming against the building's locked front doors until they burst open. Hordes of schoolchildren made their way out through the school gates, and spilled out onto the main road. There, they began intimidating pedestrians and weaving in and out of traffic. Soon all the vehicles on the road had shuddered to a complete stop. Children jumped onto car bonnets, and pulled off wing mirrors and hood ornaments. The terrified motorists locked their doors and cowered down beneath their dashboards. Sebastian hid behind the wall in the playground and looked on in abhorrence at what was happening.

When the teachers finally became aware of what was going on, they rushed outside and tried to calm the situation. But as they attempted to intervene, the children turned on them. Dozens of students stampeded in their direction, clawing and biting. And so all the teachers rushed back into the school and barricaded themselves in the staffroom. Sebastian quickly ran a short distance down the road so that he wouldn't get caught up in the violence. He looked back over his shoulder and saw David prancing about, egging on the other children as they committed random acts of recklessness. "*For shame, David...*" Sebastian thought, very disappointed with his friend. The situation showed no sign of abating, and so he decided that it would be best to get the bus home.

His bus had to stop as a group of children stood defiantly in the middle of the road, but eventually it was allowed to continue on its way. Back at his house, Sebastian ate his microwave dinner and then, ignoring the advice of the social workers who had visited him, he did some cleaning. When his parents arrived in from work, he told them about the riot at school. However, they didn't seem particularly surprised by the news, and told their son that such incidents had been happening all over the city recently. When eight o'clock came, everything across the city fell into darkness as the government shut off the electricity and gas for the night. Sebastian wearily climbed the stairs and went to bed.

* * *

Early the next morning, Mr Howard rang Sebastian's school to see if it was still open. He asked to speak to the head teacher, and after a few seconds he was put through to Mr Wallace. He questioned him about the riot, and Mr Wallace confirmed that there had indeed been a small incident yesterday but said that classes would resume as normal today. He added that the teachers had held a meeting to discuss the best course of action regarding the disturbance, and had decided to implement some big changes at the school. Mr Howard said he hoped that the children who had taken part in the riot would be appropriately reprimanded, but Mr Wallace informed him that punishing them wouldn't address the "root cause" of the problem. As the two men debated the merits of punishing badly behaved children, it gradually became obvious to Sebastian's father that Mr Wallace couldn't be reasoned with. Feeling exasperated, he ended the phone call and left for work.

Shortly after, Sebastian also left the house, destined for school. When he arrived, he saw that the school building was in a terrible state. All the windows were smashed and Mr McHugh and Mr Redmond were in the playground, sweeping up shards of glass. Sebastian went to his classroom and sat down. Ms Joyce, who had, with the help of her union official, managed to thwart Mr Wallace's attempt to fire her, was sitting at her desk. When all the students had taken their seats, she stood up and informed the class that after yesterday's riot, all the teachers had attended a very important meeting. After careful consideration, they had realised that there are too many oppressive rules and regulations at the school, leading to pent-up frustrations in the students.

Hence, from now on, the children could show up for class at whatever time suited them. And they need not stay seated at their desks anymore; they could wander freely around the classroom. Also, the students would no longer have to go to the canteen to eat. They could now eat their lunches in the classroom, whenever they felt hungry. And instead of them being required to read the moral stories out loud to the class, Ms Joyce would read the stories to them. But, she stressed that they should all try their best to pay attention, as she would still be selecting children to explain the morals of the stories as she recorded them.

"Will Mr Redmond allow us to run in the playground from now on?" a child asked.

"No, I'm afraid that won't be possible because you could fall and injure yourselves," was her reply.

Soon the classroom was filled with the sound of banter as children roamed around uninhibited. Ms Joyce began the morning by teaching new student Stefan, English. After about an hour, the class moved on to a history lesson about the British Empire. Ms Joyce spoke at length about how dreadful the Empire was, and how terribly the British treated the poor natives in the countries they colonised. Sebastian tried his best to pay attention, but the level of noise produced by his unruly classmates was making it impossible.

As he sat idly daydreaming out the classroom window, a plan began to form in his mind. If only he could somehow change the moral lessons in the *Moral Stories for Kids* books, then maybe the other children would take heed and begin to behave better. He wondered whether it would be possible to make counterfeit books and swap them with the real books.

As the school day progressed, Sebastian began to fine-tune the plan. He could use the word processor on his home computer to write new moral stories. That is, stories that taught sensible moral values – unlike the rubbish in the real books. He could also use the computer's scan function to make copies of the front and back covers of a real book to use on the counterfeit books. Binding the books could be a problem though; although Sebastian figured he could use glue to hold them together and make spines from pieces of cardboard.

When three o'clock came, Sebastian inconspicuously grabbed one of the schoolbooks from off of Ms Joyce's desk and slipped into his schoolbag. As he walked out through the school gates, a 'Wanted' poster adorning one of the street's lampposts caught his eye. He instantly recognised the man in the picture. It was Mr Stevens! Sebastian ran over to one of the posters and read the text. It said that the former school headmaster had been caught infiltrating the rehabilitation centre after gaining a job there under a false pretence. He had been accused of plotting to lead a prisoner revolt, but had managed to escape from custody and was now on the loose. Anyone with any information was urged to ring the police.

Sebastian's mind raced as he continued on to the bus stop. Should he tell anybody that he had been privy to the fact that Mr Stevens had been illegally infiltrating the rehabilitation centre? Or should he say nothing? He reasoned out the situation and eventually concluded that he should say nothing. After all, he had promised the man that he wouldn't tell a soul about his true intent working in the centre. And anyway, who was to say that the authorities were right and Mr Stevens was wrong? Sebastian had known the headmaster for several years and had the utmost respect for him. He considered him a man of unfailing integrity and impeccable manners.

When he arrived back home, Sebastian immediately completed his homework, writing: "I thought that the moral stories we read in class today were ludicrous. No wonder my fellow students are so badly behaved when they are being taught such garbage!" In keeping with his emerging plan, he took the copy of *Moral Stories for Kids* he had swiped from school out from his schoolbag and then sat down at the computer in the living room. After scanning the front and back covers, he opened the word processor and began to write some new moral stories. They weren't anything too elaborate; just a mixture of plain common sense and moral principles he had learned from the folk stories and fairy tales he had read with his parents and Mr Stevens.

When Mr and Mrs Howard arrived home from work, Sebastian told them that Mr Stevens was a wanted criminal. However, it turned out that they already knew as they had seen news reports about his crime. They expressed surprise that the former headmaster was a fugitive criminal, as he didn't seem like the type. The Howards knew that their son would encounter Mr Stevens some mornings on his way to school and asked whether he had known anything about the man's criminal escapades in the rehabilitation centre. But Sebastian told them that he had not.

That night in bed, Sebastian found it difficult to sleep. "*Poor Mr Stevens…*" he thought, and wondered where he could be hiding in the freezing city. His mind then turned to the plan involving the schoolbooks. He wondered whether it was feasible, and more importantly, whether it was morally justified.

* * *

As Sebastian rode the bus to school the following day, he noticed an increased police presence in the city. When he got into class he chatted with David for a few minutes about the unfolding situation involving their former headmaster. David was equally shocked by the news, but took a more cynical view than Sebastian.

"I hope he's brought to justice soon," he opined.

"What!?" Sebastian spluttered, astounded that his friend would express such a view.

"I used to think he was alright too," David replied. "but the more I think about it, I realise that he's a nasty piece of work. He was always picking on that poor kid, Michael. Remember? He even had an offensive nickname for him – 'Mischievous Michael'. God only knows how badly he treated the poor prisoners in the rehabilitation centre…"

"Yes, alright, whatever…" Sebastian said in a huff, feeling very irritated with David.

Sebastian sat patiently through the day's lessons as his classmates chatted to each other and played games on their phones. During lunchtime, he sat by himself in the canteen, feeling lonely, while David talked to Becky and her friends. When class resumed, he followed along as Ms Joyce taught arithmetic and then geography. He was glad when three o'clock finally came.

CHAPTER 9

The weeks went by, and although the initially media flurry about Mr Stevens had died down, he remained at large. Sebastian had developed chronic migraines, which he believed resulted from the elevated noise level in his classroom (which occurred since the school authorities had decided to relax rules and regulations). Nevertheless, he was making good progress writing his own moral stories. Each day after school he would go to the living room and, after completing his homework, he would write some new stories. He ensured that the font size and formatting style were exactly like those in the real *Moral Stories for Kids* books. Although he rather enjoyed concocting the stories, he found the act of printing them off and compiling them into volumes somewhat tedious. Eventually, he wondered whether he should ask David to help.

At school, Sebastian found it difficult to get a moment alone with his friend. Finally, one day during lunchtime, when the two boys were sitting together in the canteen, Sebastian told David about the scheme he had devised. However, David was captivated by a talk show showing on the canteen's TV set and was barely listening, but he acknowledged that the plan seemed very ingenious. Sebastian exhaled and looked up at the television. Two downtrodden-looking guests were sitting in front of a studio audience, and the programme's presenter kept shouting at them and telling them what losers he thought they were.

"Scum, you're both scum!" he kept repeating, riling them up. Within seconds a fight broke out when one of the guests violently head-butted his companion. Security staff jumped in and pulled the two individuals apart. Sebastian waited till the adverts began playing, and when he had David's full attention, he timidly asked if he would be interested in helping put the plan into action.

"Yeah, yeah, I'll help you..." David replied casually.

Just then, the talk show resumed, once more distracting him. "Let's get Graham on the show ladies and gentleman!" exclaimed the presenter as the show's psychotherapist swaggered onto the set. But Sebastian wasn't interested and instead gazed out the window at some children in the playground who were tormenting Mr Redmond.

* * *

And so at three o'clock each day from then on, the two boys would get the bus back to Sebastian's house. After completing their homework, they'd print off the moral stories Sebastian had written and use glue to hold the pages together. They also printed onto dozens of cardboard sheets copies of the scanned front and back covers of *Moral Stories for Kids,* to be used as the covers of the counterfeit books. When they were finished each day, the boys would go upstairs to Sebastian's bedroom and hide all the partially-completed books under the bed, where his mother and father wouldn't find them. As he waited for his parents to arrive home, Sebastian would often spend some time playing Chopin on the piano. The melancholic sound of the pieces reflected his mood perfectly.

The Smiths usually rang at least once a week to talk to their friends. By now, Mr Smith had purchased a new house for his family and Adam had started back at school. Adam told Sebastian that he liked his new school – it was similar to their old school (at least in so far as the students studied things they didn't already know and the teachers maintained control over their class). When Sebastian told Adam that Mr Stevens had been accused of trying to bring about a prisoner revolt in the rehabilitation centre and was now a wanted criminal, Adam was flabbergasted.

"I hope he continues to evade capture," he said.

Sebastian also informed him about the plot with the schoolbooks, but asked him not to tell his parents about it (for he hadn't even told his own parents).

Adam loved the plan. "I wish I'd thought of that!" he said.

* * *

One blustery evening in mid-February, Mr and Mrs Howard told Sebastian that they had some exciting news. They had managed to obtain visas that would allow them go and live in the United States, and were due to depart in three weeks' time. Sebastian was delighted, but also surprised.

"How did you manage to get visas so quickly?" he asked.

But his parents didn't answer his question and instead kept telling him about how great their new life in America would be. They would transfer the last of their savings to the Smiths, who would mind the money until they arrived. The Smiths had also agreed to let them live at their new house until they got back on their feet.

Sebastian suspected that what his parents were doing was of dubious legality, so he decided not to ask them too much more about it. But as far as he was concerned, it didn't really matter anyway – they would be moving to America and he would soon be reunited with Adam!

The Howards decided to sell their furniture, including the piano and their car, rather than ship them abroad. The loss of the piano particularly bothered Sebastian, but he reasoned that it was a small price to pay to be able to leave the country. Mrs Howard rang the local council and implored them to delay demolishing their house for a little while longer; until after they had emigrated. After begging them for almost an hour, the council eventually agreed.

In bed that night, Sebastian considered whether it was worth continuing with the scheme involving the schoolbooks. He quickly concluded that it was. David was involved now and he felt that he would be letting him down if he discontinued it. Either way, the new moral stories would hopefully change some of the children in their class for the better, which was after all the plan's ultimate aim. But the family's scheduled departure in three weeks did mean that David and he were under time pressure to finish the new books.

* * *

The following day at school, Sebastian told everyone that he would be emigrating.

"Aww, no! I'll miss you so much mate," David stated loudly, throwing his arms around his friend.

"We'll all be so devastated when you leave!" Becky shouted out.

"Yes, you certainly made some very interesting contributions to our class, Sebastian," Ms Joyce said, and then began the morning's lessons.

* * *

Each day, whenever he got the chance, Sebastian read the newspapers and watched television news stations to follow any developments in the hunt for Mr Stevens. Although there were occasional alleged sightings of him in the city, there was no tangible evidence as to his whereabouts. David and Sebastian continued to work hard each afternoon making the fake books so they could implement their plan before Sebastian left.

* * *

The week before the Howards were due to leave, Sebastian saw very little of his parents. When they came home from work each day they spent several hours doing paperwork and making phone calls (trying to ensure that everything went smoothly with their new life abroad).

School progressed as usual and the only incident of note occurred one lunchtime as the children were eating in the canteen. Mr Wallace made an announcement over the school intercom. He said that he would shortly be retiring from the post of school head teacher to take up another job. He added that he had thoroughly enjoyed his time working at the school and was proud of all that he had accomplished during his tenure.

"Good riddance!" Sebastian mumbled under his breath, and then went back to eating his lunch as children around him screamed and fought each other.

* * *

On Tuesday, the second-last day before his scheduled departure, David and Sebastian spent much of the afternoon putting the finishing touches on the books. They made spines from strips of cardboard and carefully stuck them onto each book. The boys were very happy with the final products. To the naked eye the counterfeit books appeared to be exactly the same as the real books; the only difference being the moral stories within. The boys each packed half of the books into their schoolbags and then finalised their plan of action. They agreed that they would walk out of their classroom together, set off the school's fire alarm, and hide in the toilets. When everyone had evacuated the building, they would sneak back into their classroom and swap the schoolbooks with the counterfeit ones. It was after four o'clock when David left, and Sebastian sat down in the living room and turned on the television.

Fed-up with the dire quality of the programmes, he began to flick through the stations. He tuned to a news station that was reporting on a breaking story. It said that Mr Stevens had recently been spotted near one of the city's airports, and police suspected that he was attempting to stow away on a plane. The reporter said the net was closing in on him, but warned that he was extremely dangerous and advised all citizens to be on high alert.

Sebastian sat up and looked at the clock on the living room wall (as he still hadn't found his missing watch). It was now 4.20p.m. After pondering for a few minutes, he decided to get the bus to the airport and look for Mr Stevens. If he found him, maybe he could harbour him in his house until himself and his parents left, or even help him flee the country. It was a long shot, but still worth a try. Although Sebastian had promised his parents that he would never wander around the city by himself, this was clearly an exceptional situation.

And so he left the house and made his way to the bus stop and looked at the bus timetable. Once he identified the bus that went to the airport, he waited patiently. Eventually the bus came and he climbed on board. A gang of thuggish-looking youths were sitting down at the back, devouring a takeaway meal, and so Sebastian took a seat near the driver. The young hoodlums hurled abuse and threw chips at other passengers, but nobody dared reprimand them. Sebastian knew not to stare at them, lest he attract their unwanted attention. Eventually the bus approached the stop near the airport and Sebastian alighted. 'Wanted' posters of Mr Stevens were everywhere, and armed police officers paced back and forth along the streets.

Sebastian had only walked a few steps when there was loud honking of car horns. He looked around and saw an elderly lady slowly making her way across the road. Impatient drivers were beeping furiously and screaming at her to hurry up. Sebastian dashed over and helped her across the street.

"Thank you," she said disconcertedly.

But a group of pedestrians rapidly formed around Sebastian and pulled him away from the woman. A young college student carrying a rucksack started to scold him for what he had done. "That type of behaviour constitutes ageism," he said. "You should treat the elderly the same way you would treat anybody else."

Sebastian knew that he would be wasting his time trying to argue with the arrogant student, so he said nothing and just continued on his way.

He wandered around the dirty city streets, scanning the face of each person who walked past, looking for Mr Stevens.

"What the hell are you staring at!?" one man shouted when their eyes met. Sebastian paced through the thoroughfares near the airport for hours, searching for his former headmaster, but without any success. The city's tall buildings cast dark shadows as the pale winter sun disappeared behind them. As the daylight faded and the temperature dropped, instead of the city becoming more desolate, to Sebastian's surprise it was becoming busier.

Dozens of young people poured onto the streets and began frolicking about. A group of women wearing high heels and miniskirts pointed at Sebastian.

"Look at the midget!" they giggled.

Sebastian informed them that he was not a midget, but actually a little boy. The women staggered towards him in a stupor, but he managed to scamper away. As he turned a corner, he noticed a man standing outside, urinating against the wall. He stopped and stared, shocked that someone would urinate so brazenly in public.

"You shouldn't piddle in the street," he said admonishingly.

"You have no right to criticise me you little brat!" the man roared.

Sebastian began to feel fearful and decided that it might be best not to talk to anybody else. But a little further on up the street, he noticed a girl lying motionless in a gutter. People were walking past, apparently oblivious to her. He leaned over her to get a better look. Concerned that she might have been the victim of an assault, he reached down and gently shook her. The girl began to stir and gradually came to her senses. "What the…?" she suddenly cried out. "This guy is trying to touch me!"

"Oh no, I was just checking that you are alright," Sebastian said. A crowd of drunken louts began to gather around, attracted by the girl's cries.

"Pervert!" someone shouted. One of the louts tried to grab hold of Sebastian, but in his drunkenness he lost his footing and plummeted to the ground.

"I'll kill you!" he shouted as he clambered to his feet.

Sebastian took off at speed. He rushed up to a policeman who was standing by his motorcycle.

"Excuse me! A man is threatening to kill me!" he said frantically. But no sooner had he the words out of his mouth when a crackly voice sounded over the policeman's radio. It said that a report had just been received about some shady-looking characters drunkenly singing and dancing in a nearby (smokeless) coal yard. The policeman's face turned ashen. He immediately leapt onto the motorcycle and fumbled frantically to get the keys into the ignition. Then the wail of a siren reverberated through the air as he zoomed off into the distance, leaving a smell of burning rubber in his wake.

Sebastian felt terrified and wished he had never bothered coming into the city to look for Mr Stevens. He took refuge in a dark alcove beneath a railway bridge and made sure to stand well back from the giant cobwebs that hung from the structure's ceiling. As he was contemplating whether he should just go home, all the streetlights suddenly went off and everything fell into darkness. For a few seconds he felt like he was blind, but his eyes slowly adjusted to the dimness. After several moments of eerie silence, the sound of laughing and talking resumed. Everywhere, people began lighting bonfires and feeding the flames with heaps of rubbish.

Gradually the sound of voices increased in volume and then turned into frenzied screams. Sebastian walked to the end of the railway bridge and peeped around the corner. In the shadowy street he could see a large baying mob of men, women and children. Right in the centre of the mob was Mr Stevens! He had scratches on his face and his pinstriped suit was torn and tattered. People threw punches and spat at him. Sebastian could see the fear in Mr Stevens' eyes as he scrambled on his hands and knees, desperately trying to get away from the angry vigilantes. Sebastian rushed over and attempted to get to his former headmaster, but he was unable to fight his way through the crowd.

Within minutes, the blue flashing lights of police cars illuminated the scene. Mr Stevens managed to break free from the mob and bolted off down an alleyway – with several heavily-armed police officers in hot pursuit. A sudden burst of machinegun-fire echoed throughout the streets, and then an unnerving silence descended. The mob gathered at the entrance of the alleyway, but the police put up a cordon and began to push everyone back.

Sebastian was in a panicked state, unsure whether Mr Stevens had been injured or even killed. He couldn't see through the thick crowd and frantically asked bystanders if they knew what was happening.

"I think he's been shot!" a woman said.

After a few minutes an ambulance arrived and the paramedics lifted the former headmaster in through the back doors. The vehicle then sped off with its siren wailing.

By now Sebastian was in a blind panic. He took off towards the bus station at full speed, bolting straight through the numerous puddles of vomit on the ground. He climbed aboard a bus that was just about to depart, and fumbled around in his trouser pocket looking for his bus card.

"Come on, come on!" the bus driver said impatiently.

When he had paid his fare, the bus set off on the homeward journey. He crouched down in his seat and began hyperventilating, trying desperately not to draw attention to himself. When the bus finally arrived at the stop near his home, he hopped off and ran the short distance back to his house.

There, Sebastian found his parents waiting for him, wondering where he had been. Through his sobs, he explained what had happened. Their initial reaction was one of shock and sadness, but then Mr Howard began to grow angry at his son.

"Do you have any idea how dangerous the city is after dusk?!" he yelled. "Don't you realise that you could have been mugged, or assaulted, or worse?" Sebastian's father stormed up the stairs and into his bedroom, slamming the door behind him.

Sebastian began to cry harder. Mrs Howard put her arms around her son to comfort him, but reiterated that he should *not* have wandered around the city by himself.

She then told him to go to his room and that she would bring him up a warm drink. A few minutes later, Sebastian was in bed and sipping from a cup of hot chocolate. However, he was still upset and kept thinking about everything that had happened. His parents checked on him several times throughout the night and tried to provide comfort by downplaying the seriousness of Mr Stevens' situation. But Sebastian didn't sleep a wink and spent the entire night weeping.

* * *

At 8.00a.m. he rushed downstairs to the living room. He flicked through the television stations until he found a news programme. The news anchor said that the fugitive, Mr Stevens, had been shot and killed last night during a confrontation with armed police. Sebastian felt a cold chill run through his entire body. His parents stood by his side and tried to console him, but to no avail. He was too grief-stricken to eat any breakfast, and just sat motionless at the kitchen table with his head bowed.

Mrs Howard tried to persuade Sebastian to stay at home that day, but he insisted on going to school. It was his last day before they moved, and he wanted to say his goodbyes to David. He felt extremely gloomy as he rode the bus into school that morning, and everything looked blurred through his tearful eyes. He spent the entire bus journey thinking about his former headmaster. But slowly Sebastian's sadness was replaced by a feeling of fortitude. He reasoned that although the past couldn't be changed, the future could. He was going to implement the plan with the schoolbooks today no matter what! If Mr Stevens had known about the plot, he would surely have approved. After all, he had also detested the moral story schoolbooks. Sebastian alighted from the bus and marched to school with a stoical attitude. The first thing he did when he got into class was to tell David the heart-breaking news about their former headmaster.

"Yes, I already heard. It's so tragic, isn't it?" David replied.

CHAPTER 10

Despite his valiant mind-set, nervousness was beginning to get the better of Sebastian. Throughout the school day, he kept procrastinating and procrastinating. He watched on in silence as Ms Joyce taught English to new student, Stefan, and then feebly participated as the class read some moral stories. Eventually, during a maths lesson, when there was only about one hour of the school day remaining, he nudged David with his elbow. It was now or never. The two boys stood up and walked hurriedly out of the class; nobody seemed to notice them leave. They walked along the corridor until they came to a fire alarm. 'Break glass in case of emergency' the instructions read. They looked back and forth along the corridor and, once the coast was clear, David clenched his fist and punched his knuckles into the alarm, smashing the glass. Immediately, the alarm rang loudly throughout the whole school.

The two boys quickly ran into the toilets and hid in one of the cubicles. Back in their classroom, Ms Joyce was overcome with panic.

"Quick everybody, get out!" she screamed at the top of her lungs. However, few of the children in the class paid her much attention. Tyrone began to dance to the sound of the ringing alarm, much to the amusement of his sister. Ms Joyce ran about the room in an agitated state, desperately trying to escort all her students towards the door. She was careful not to make physical contact with any of them though, lest it be construed as assault.

Eventually, after about 20 minutes, all the school's staff and students had gathered in the playground.

When the sound of voices had faded, Sebastian and David made their way back into their classroom. They picked up their schoolbags and crept towards Ms Joyce's desk, upon which sat the moral story schoolbooks in neat stacks. As Sebastian reached out towards the stacks his heart began to race and his hand started to shake. The boys quickly went about unpacking the counterfeit books from their schoolbags and swapping them with the real ones. As the fire alarm continued to sound, they kept glancing towards the classroom door every few seconds to make sure they weren't being watched.

Just as they were finishing swapping the books, a voice suddenly asked, "What are you doing?" The boys jumped with fright. Peeping in through the doorway was Becky.

David became flustered "We're just uh… uh…"

Becky strode over to where the boys were standing and snatched a fake book out of Sebastian's hand. As she looked through it, the two boys desperately tried to think of something to say to explain away the whole situation. But it seemed the game was up.

"Look Becky…" Sebastian said. "Basically, we made some new schoolbooks and we are replacing them with the real ones."

"Why?" Becky asked, looking genuinely mystified. Sebastian explained to Becky his belief that their schoolbooks provide very bad moral lessons, hence the naughty behaviour of most the children in their class.

Becky flicked her long red hair and gave the boys a big smile. "I understand. Well, don't worry guys," she said, "your secret is safe with me." Sebastian put the last of the real books into his schoolbag and zipped it up. Suddenly, the alarm stopped ringing and the children began to flow back into the classroom. Sebastian, David, and Becky quickly blended in with the stream of returning children.

"It was just a false alarm" Ms Joyce kept reassuring everyone.

By now it was three o'clock and time for everybody to go home. Everyone gathered up their belongings and headed for the school's exit. David and Sebastian walked through the corridor, past the secretary's desk and out into the car park.

"I hope we can trust Becky" Sebastian whispered to his friend.

"We can, definitely. She's really nice," David replied confidently.

Becky saw the two boys chatting, and sensing that they were talking about her, skipped over to them. "I just want to reassure you two that I definitely won't tell anybody that you swapped the schoolbooks. It would be terrible if anyone were to find out. The police would take a crime like that very seriously and would probably even offer a reward for information leading to the apprehension of the culprits."

"Well, I don't know about that!" Sebastian said with a laugh, doubtful that the police would care too much about a few schoolbooks, when they barely seemed bothered when a man tried to attack him or when Adam's house got burgled. The three children chatted for a few minutes, and when David commented that he was feeling hungry and should get going, Becky immediately invited him back to her house for supper. He was hesitant at first, but Becky was very persevering, and after pleading with him for a few minutes, he caved in.

Just before David and Becky parted ways with Sebastian, David turned back to his friend. "I guess I won't see you again before you emigrate Sebastian," he said.

"I guess not," Sebastian replied. "My parents and I are scheduled to depart on an early flight in the morning." He thanked David for all his help making the counterfeit schoolbooks and promised that he would keep in touch.

"Goodbye Sebastian," Becky said, shaking his hand. "I hope your mental problems clear up soon. Always remember, mental illness is nothing to be ashamed of…"

"Yes, alright, goodbye Becky" Sebastian replied.

Sebastian staggered to the bus stop, weighed down by his heavy schoolbag. When the bus eventually arrived, it battled its way through the city's heavy traffic until it reached the stop near Sebastian's house. Sebastian knew that his parents would still be at work, and rather than be all alone in his house, he decided to go for a walk in the park. He walked in through the graffiti-covered arch at the park's entrance, and headed towards the pond. Much to his dismay, the park had become even dirtier than last time he'd been there. A horrible smell emanated from the pond's stagnant water and there was no wildlife to be seen anywhere. Sebastian walked along the path, carefully stepping over discarded syringes and empty cans of lager. He then sat down on a bench and rested.

He could hear the faint cooing of a wood pigeon in some nearby trees. But a few seconds later the cooing was drowned out by the sound of ear-splitting music. He looked around and saw a gang of hoodie-clad yobs walking along the footpath, blasting a song by pop singer Billie Piper from a stereo.

"*Why you gotta play that song so loud? Because we want to, because we want to!*" sang Billie.

The gang started cavorting near where Sebastian was sitting, causing a ruckus.

Unable to relax, he walked over to a park warden who was standing idly by the park railings and politely asked if he could move the gang along. "They have as much right to be here as you do," the warden replied crossly. Feeling disgruntled, Sebastian decided that he might as well go home. At least he would get some peace and quiet there. He trudged the quarter of a mile or so to his street and noticed that bulldozers and JCBs were demolishing the row of houses on the road. In fact, there was only one house that was still fully intact – his own. It would be demolished tomorrow, but by then Sebastian and his parents would be thousands of miles away in America.

As Sebastian walked towards his home, he stopped momentarily near where the Smiths' house had once stood. Now there was just a huge pile of rubble and debris. A couple of smashed toys lay on the ground underneath where Adam's bedroom had been, while his mangled tree house was strewn about by the trunk of the oak tree in the back garden. Sebastian felt nostalgic as he thought about the numerous times himself and his best friend had played together in the house and tree house, and eaten cookies made by Adam's mother. Just as he was about to continue walking, he noticed a bright red object perched on top of a remaining piece of the house wall. He looked closer and realised that it was the stuffed dragon that Adam had bought in the park on his birthday. It sat perfectly upright and looked surprisingly intact and clean. The reptilian had a sinister grin on its face and a forked tongue protruded from its mouth. It struck Sebastian as odd that the toy dragon should survive the demolition unscathed, and he assumed that one of the demolition workers had propped it up on the wall in jest.

He continued on to his own house and let himself in. The hallway was full of suitcases packed with clothes and other necessities. Other than that, the house was relatively bare, a result of Mr and Mrs Howard selling most of the furniture. Only a few items such as their beds, a couple of chairs, the microwave, and a television remained. Sebastian immediately went up to his room and threw his schoolbag containing the appropriated schoolbooks under his bed so that they would be destroyed in the demolition the next day.

When he came back downstairs, he went to the kitchen and put a ready-made meal in the microwave. He set the timer and watched as the little dish of ham and turkey slowly rotated in the machine. The food wasn't a patch on his mother's homemade cooking, but he never complained. He was well aware that his family were in dire straits. At any rate, Sebastian wasn't particularly hungry this afternoon. He kept thinking about the stunt David and himself had pulled at school today and imagining what life would be like in America. Moreover, the ground beneath him was constantly vibrating as the bulldozers and JCBs went about demolishing neighbouring houses. Nevertheless, he forced himself to eat most of his dinner.

He sat in the living room and turned on the television just as a talk show was starting. A female guest was sitting on the stage beside the programme's presenter. She wore a black cloth covering her head and face.

"Would you like to tell us your story?" the presenter asked her.

The woman composed herself and began. "My parents forced me to marry a very violent man who regularly beat me and treated me like a slave. Then one day when he was particularly angry, he threw acid in my face." With that, the guest removed the cloth covering revealing her badly disfigured face. The left side of her head and neck was covered in deep scarring and one of her eye sockets was hollow. The audience gasped.

"And did the police arrest your husband?" the presenter asked. "No," the woman replied, "I begged them to arrest him but they still haven't."

"Let's hear from someone in our audience," the presenter continued, handing a microphone to a young man sitting in the front row.

The man stood up and put the mic to his mouth. "There's all this talk 'bout the guest being ugly or somethin', but I just wanna say, I think she's beautiful! She's beautiful!" he declared in an extraordinary display of moral exhibitionism. The audience erupted into applause. The woman tried to respond, but could barely be heard over all the clapping.

"Why will no one help me?" she sobbed.

Sebastian turned off the television, dismayed by what he had just witnessed. "*So very sad…*" he thought. With nothing else to do, he just sat idly on the staircase, waiting for his parents to return from work. When they eventually arrived home, they greeted their son and gave him a big hug. They all agreed that they were excited at the thought of emigrating tomorrow.

While Mr and Mrs Howard were packing away the last of the family's belongings, the telephone rang. Sebastian rushed into the kitchen and answered it.

"Hi Sebastian, its Adam," said a familiar voice.

"I can't wait to see you tomorrow!" Sebastian blurted out with excitement. The line was poor, but Sebastian told his friend about the demolition of his house and destruction of his tree house.

"That's a pity," Adam replied solemnly. "We'll have to get working on a new tree house when you get here."

As the boys continued to speak, the line became crackly and then went dead. About two minutes later, the phone rang again and Sebastian again picked up. "Adam?" he asked. He could hear Adam talking, but his voice sounded muffled and the phone line hissed with static. When the line again went dead, Sebastian hung up. He waited by the phone for 15 minutes, but Adam didn't ring back.

As always, the gas and electricity shut off at eight o'clock, and so Sebastian lit a candle and climbed the stairs. After using the bathroom, he went into his bedroom and got undressed. Glancing out his bedroom window, he noticed that the atmosphere was even darker than usual due to a low lying blanket of cloud hanging over the city, blocking out the moonlight. Shadowy buildings jutted awkwardly towards the sky, giving the city a menacing and creepy ambiance.

The only bright light to be seen emanated from the rehabilitation centre, which shone like a beacon in the distance. Sebastian was glad that, as of tomorrow, he would never have to see the dismal city again. He pulled down the blinds, blew out the candle, and lay down. Although he was tired, he couldn't sleep. He kept thinking about Mr Stevens' tragic demise. Then, after a while, his thoughts turned to the stunt that David and he had pulled at school that day. He wondered what the children in his class would think of the new stories in their schoolbooks. Would they think them silly? Would they even understand the moral lessons? Sebastian just lay in the darkness, thinking and shivering.

Eventually, he heard the sound of his parents making their way upstairs. They gently creaked open his bedroom door and told him that he should try and get some sleep. A taxi was scheduled to collect them early in the morning and take them to the airport. They had a long day of travel ahead of them tomorrow. The wind began to gust outside and sleety rain started to fall. Sebastian closed his eyes and hugged his pillow. Then he remembered that the necklace his mother had given him for safekeeping was still hidden beneath one of the bedroom's floorboard, but he was feeling too cold to retrieve it. "*I'll get it in the morning before we leave...*" he thought as he slowly nodded off.

Sebastian had been asleep for a few hours when he suddenly sat up in the bed with a jolt. There had just been a strange noise outside. He knew that the city was crawling with thieves, gangsters, and drug addicts, and after the experience with the burglar at Adam's house, he wasn't going to take any chances. He went over to the window and was just reaching out to pull open the blinds when there was an enormous crash downstairs. The front door had been smashed in and a freezing gust of wind blew through the house. Sebastian could hear shouting and the clamour of footsteps on the hall tiles, which then hurriedly began making their way up the stairs. Within seconds, his bedroom door flew open and several heavily armed policemen burst in. Red laser beams from their rifles darted around the room and quickly localised on Sebastian's body.

"Stay down!" one of the men screamed.

But Sebastian couldn't move anyway; he was paralysed by fear.

An officer jumped on top of Sebastian, pinning him to the floor. He pressed his knee down on Sebastian's back and handcuffed his arms behind him, causing Sebastian to wail in agony. Sebastian was then dragged, still in his pyjamas, down the stairs and out through front door. There was a police car parked just outside the house, its blue flashing lights illuminating the otherwise dark and desolate street.

He could hear the agitated cries of his parents who had run out into the freezing night behind him. "Where are you taking our son!?" Mr Howard screamed.

"What's happening? What's happening?" his wife kept asking frantically.

Sebastian was quickly bundled into the back of the police car, which immediately took off at full speed.

"Why are you arresting me?!" he asked as he squirmed against the handcuffs. "We know about the schoolbooks, Sebastian…" one of the policemen snapped. The police car raced through the bleak early morning streets, skidding around corners. After a few minutes it reached the police station. Sebastian was taken into an interrogation room and read his rights. A police sergeant placed a stack of the counterfeit schoolbooks on the desk, and even in the faint candlelight, Sebastian could see the anger in his eyes. He picked up one of the books and began to leaf through it. "Never before have I seen such disgusting filth," he muttered, looking at Sebastian with a cold stare. The sergeant began to read one of the stories out loud, but within seconds his voice cracked with emotion and he broke down in tears.

"I can't read any more. It's too horrendous," he snivelled. The other officers gathered around and tried to comfort him.

Sebastian was then led into another room where an old, overweight man was waiting for him. He wore a suit and bow-tie, and horned-rimmed glasses. The man introduced himself as Mr Jenkins and said that he would be acting as Sebastian's legal representative. Sebastian immediately asked if he could see his parents, but Mr Jenkins informed him that this wasn't possible. His parents were currently being questioned at another police station to determine what role, if any, they had in the crime.

"Did they know about the fake schoolbooks?" Mr Jenkins asked.

"No," Sebastian replied truthfully.

Mr Jenkins provided Sebastian with a change of clothes, which consisted of a pair of jeans and a sweatshirt, and then told him to have a seat as there were some important things that they needed to discuss.

They sat down together at a small table in the centre of the room. "How did the police find out?" Sebastian asked.

"I believe your friend David informed them," Mr Jenkins replied. Sebastian's jaw dropped. Then he felt his temperature rise and his blood begin to boil. He was shocked that David would betray him. "The police had your house under surveillance most of yesterday evening and last night. They even tapped your phone," the legal expert said as he opened his briefcase and pulled out a morning newspaper. "And to make matters worse, David's been blabbering to the press," he continued, placing the newspaper down on the table right in front of Sebastian.

The headline consisted of just two words, 'Hate Crime', and accompanying the text was a photograph of Sebastian. His blood ran cold as he read down through the article. It said that he was a loner with no friends and that he had mental problems…

"Listen to me Sebastian," Mr Jenkins said, prompting him to look up from the newspaper. "You have offended a lot of people with this deed involving the schoolbooks."

"I-I-know," Sebastian stuttered nervously.

Mr Jenkins then gave him a stern look and informed him that given the seriousness of the offence, he would be going to trial immediately.

But he assured Sebastian that he would do everything in his power to help him beat the charges.

"Now, I understand that you have been diagnosed with mental problems?" Mr Jenkins asked, peering intensely over his glasses.

"Yes, yes… a psychologist diagnosed me with Oppositional Defiant Disorder and Attention Deficit Disorder," Sebastian replied.

"Okay then, you are going to plead not guilty. Our main argument will be that you're too young to be held accountable for your actions. If that doesn't work, you can plead not guilty by reason of insanity," Mr Jenkins said.

"And if that doesn't work?" Sebastian asked, growing increasingly worried.

Mr Jenkins thought for a moment.

"Then I suppose we'll just try to blame the whole thing on David," he replied.

Sebastian carefully considered the legal expert's advice and asked him whether that was really an ethical thing to do.

"Oh, who cares!?" Mr Jenkins said with a laugh. "After all, he ratted you out." Mr Jenkins chatted with Sebastian for a few more minutes, explaining some legal issues and technicalities. Sebastian felt foggy-headed but tried his best to focus on what Mr Jenkins told him.

Soon it was time for Sebastian to leave the police station and head for the courthouse. By now it was daylight and a slight mist had descended on the city. Sebastian was again bundled back into the police car and driven the short distance to the court building. A group of journalists took photographs and shouted questions as policemen led him into the court building. The officers guided him down a flight of stairs and into a holding cell. The cell was dark and murky, a layer of green moss covered the walls, and the smell of urine hung in the air. Sebastian looked around and saw a shadowy figure leaning against the cell's back wall. He immediately recognised him. It was Pete Branden, the burglar who had broken into Adam's house and attacked Mr Smith.

Sebastian' pulse began to race and he started to sweat profusely. He quickly sunk back into the shadows in the corner of the room and kept his head down, hoping the burglar wouldn't recognise him.

"So, what are you charged with kid?" Pete asked as he stumbled around the cell, inebriated. Given the apparent seriousness of his offence, Sebastian decided to fib that he had committed what he felt would be perceived as a lesser crime. Trying his best to sound poised, he said that he had been charged with assault using a deadly weapon. The burglar seemed enthralled, and in turn, Sebastian inquired what crime he had been charged with.

"Well, it's a funny story really..." Pete began, his speech slurred. "Last time I was here I was charged with burglary and assault. I gave the judge a sob story about how hard my life is and he let me off, but after the trial I followed him home to his big mansion. I broke in that night and stole his credit cards. Then I went on a spending spree!"

Sebastian pretended that that he was impressed by what the burglar had just told him. "That's awesome!" he said with a feigned laugh.

"Hopefully I'll just get a slap on the wrist," said Pete optimistically.

Sebastian and Pete chatted for a while with the burglar reminiscing about the hundreds of crimes he had committed throughout his life. All the while, Sebastian sat in the shadows with his head down, desperate not be recognised. But after listening about the burglar's extensive history of criminal activities, he began to grow optimistic that the judiciary might be lenient on him regarding his own criminal deed.

Eventually there was a rattling of keys, and the cell door opened. Two police officers stood there looking in. "Come along Sebastian!" one of them shouted.

"Good luck!" Pete said as the police led Sebastian back up the flight of stairs and into the courtroom. Sebastian began to feel jittery again and beads of cold sweat started dripping down his face. The portrait of the man with the white hair and bushy beard loomed ominously from behind the judge's bench and Sebastian could feel his eyes follow him around the room.

He took his place in the dock and looked around the packed court. People were leering at him and chattering, and he strained to hear what they were saying. A group of men sitting at the front of the gallery were calmly discussing whether Sebastian's crime could justify the return of capital punishment. A woman sat near them looked feverish. She kept staring at Sebastian with a look of terror on her face. "He's a monster!" she suddenly cried out.

Towards the back of the public gallery, Sebastian could see a couple waving frantically. It was his parents. A policewoman stood beside them, preventing them from rushing over to him. They were shouting, trying to tell him something, but he couldn't make out what they were saying. But at any rate, he was greatly relieved to see them.

A hush descended on the court as Judge Charlie walked out from his chambers. He didn't look as friendly as the last time Sebastian saw him. He had a scowl on his face and his eyes were bloodshot. As he took his seat, he slammed legal documents down on the judicial bench. After the hate crime charges against Sebastian were read out, Judge Charlie asked him how he pled. Sebastian took a deep breath and composed himself. "Not guilty," he replied, trying to sound confident. The judge then read some excerpts from the moral stories he had written. Everyone sitting in the public gallery gasped in horror. Thereafter, it was Mr Jenkins' turn to speak. The legal expert stood up and outlined the defence argument, which was that, at 10 years of age, Sebastian was too young to be held accountable for his actions.

"I don't care about his damn age!" Judge Charlie yelled, banging his fists on the bench. "Given the severity of his crime, I have decided that the defendant will be tried as an adult," he said in a fluster as he leafed through some legal documents. Mr Jenkins then informed Judge Charlie that Sebastian had been diagnosed with mental problems and thus wasn't of sound mind. The judge suddenly stopped fidgeting with his papers and looked over at Sebastian. "Oh yes, I am well aware of his mental problems. You're a very sick little boy, aren't you Sebastian?" he said, a malevolent smile slowly forming on his face.

"No!" Sebastian replied defiantly. Mr Jenkins coughed loudly.

"Umm, yes I mean," Sebastian said, correcting himself.

The various legal professionals argued throughout the day. Sebastian tried his best to follow the proceedings, but found the whole thing confusing and overwhelming. All the while, he remained conscious of the dozens of people in the court staring at him. Mr and Mrs Howard spent most of the trial holding handkerchiefs to their eyes, wiping away tears. At one point, Mrs Howard blew her son a kiss and mouthed, "I love you."

"I love you too," Sebastian mouthed back, his own eyes welling up.

During the recesses, Mr Jenkins chatted with his client and tried to explain everything to him in a way that that he could understand. He offered Sebastian a light snack, but he was too sick with worry to eat. Sebastian repeatedly asked when he would get to tell his side of the story, but Mr Jenkins just kept telling him to be patient. Things dragged on into the afternoon, and by four o'clock, he was feeling weary.

When a witness was eventually called, Sebastian perked up. Everyone in the packed court turned around as the doors opened and a young boy walked in. It was David! Sebastian began to grind his teeth and breathe heavily.

David looked very sheepish as he walked towards the front of the courtroom, and he kept his eyes fixed firmly on the floor. Court staff helped him up into the witness box and adjusted the microphone for him.

Judge Charlie turned to David. "I understand that you have something very important to tell the court," he said.

David looked uncomfortable as he glanced out over the congregation, but cleared his throat and began. "Sebastian made the fake schoolbooks all by himself and swapped them with the real ones. I tried to talk him out of it, but he wouldn't listen to me."

"That's a lie!" Sebastian screeched.

"Don't worry, I believe you," Judge Charlie said with a grin as he handed David some sweets. "You're a very good little boy David. You did the right thing by testifying against your friend."

David gave a big smile. "Oh, and another thing," he said. "The day after Sebastian was diagnosed with his mental problems, he stopped taking his medication."

"Is that right?" Judge Charlie replied, tut-tutting as he looked back towards Sebastian.

Sebastian shook with rage. He glared at David as he left the witness stand, but David kept his head down and didn't return his gaze.

By now, Sebastian was feeling incensed. He still hadn't been allowed to explain to the court why he had made the counterfeit schoolbooks. He looked towards Judge Charlie and began to speak, but the judge immediately roared at him. "Shut up! I'm not interested in anything you have to say. Is it any wonder that so many people burgle and thieve when spoilt brats like you have so much and they have so little!?" Sebastian just stood in the dock dumbfounded, but the judge continued his rant. "I go out of my way to reform criminals, only to see greedy pigs like you undo all my good work." And there's more! Look at this!" Judge Charlie continued, holding up some sheets of paper. They were Sebastian's homework exercises that the prosecution had obtained from Ms Joyce. "You find the stories in your schoolbooks silly and ridiculous, do you?!" he yelled, waving the pages furiously. "Society provides you with an excellent education, and this is the thanks you give?!"

Judge Charlie then stormed out of the courtroom and into his chambers to decide on a verdict. Mr Jenkins hurried over to Sebastian in the dock. "Don't worry, everything's going to be just fine!" he said patronisingly. Sebastian could feel his blood begin to boil again, and was about to give his legal representative a piece of his mind when Judge Charlie walked back out from his quarters. He took his seat, turned towards the dock, and looked Sebastian directly in the eye.

"I find you guilty as charged!" he said in an angry growl. Sebastian's whole body trembled from head to toe.

"Noooo!!!" Mrs Howard screamed, jumping up from her seat. Sebastian father grimaced and closed his eyes.

"Hush there!" Judge Charlie said, pointing towards the gallery. He then said that Sebastian would be sentenced in the morning and told the police to take him back down to the holding cells. Sebastian looked towards the area of the gallery where his parents had been sitting, but everyone was leaving and he couldn't see them through the crowd. As he was being brought out of the courtroom, Sebastian glanced back towards Mr Jenkins, but the legal representative just shrugged his shoulders and began to pack away his documents.

While being led down the stairs, he passed Pete Branden being led up for his own trial (he was due to be tried by another magistrate, given that it was Judge Charlie that he stood accused of thieving from). Sebastian pressed up close against the police officer leading him, so that Pete wouldn't see his face.

"Haha! You must've been found guilty if they're bringing you back down here!" Pete sneered. "Enjoy your stay in the rehabilitation centre!"

Sebastian choked up, and tears streamed from his eyes, down his cheeks and splashed onto the concrete steps. "Please let me see my mummy and daddy," he begged as the police officer led him back into the holding cell.

But the officer didn't acquiesce to Sebastian's plea or offer any comfort. "I hope you're happy with all the trouble you've caused," he commented as he closed and locked the cell door.

As Sebastian stood alone in the cell, he started to panic. He felt dizzy and wheezed with each breath he took. The cell walls looked like they were closing in on him and the sound of Pete Branden's hideous laughter kept ringing in his ears. Suddenly, everything went black.

For a few seconds after he came round, Sebastian didn't know where he was, but he gradually came back to his senses. His surroundings remained enveloped in darkness and back of his head was throbbing. He put his hand to it and under his hair he could feel a bump where he had banged his head on the ground when he collapsed. He had no idea how long he'd been unconscious, and couldn't tell if the darkness was due to the trauma to his head or the electricity having been switched off.

With no visual cues, it was difficult for him to keep track of time. He huddled up against the wall and, slightly concussed, spent much of the night hovering between sleep and consciousness. Just as he was beginning to wonder whether the whole trial had been a bad dream, he heard a man's voice shout "Sebastian!"

Startled, he opened his eyes expecting to see his father. But instead he saw a police officer standing by the door, ready to take him back upstairs for his sentencing.

In the packed courtroom, Mr and Mrs Howard were once again seated in the gallery, looking grief-stricken. As Sebastian took his place in the dock, Judge Charlie walked out from his chambers.

After discussing some legalities, he turned to Sebastian. "Given the public outrage at your crime, I have no choice but to sentence you to 25 years of intensive rehabilitation."

"Oh my God! Oh my God!" Sebastian kept repeating, and threw his cusped hands up to his face.

"This is a travesty!" Mr Howard shouted from the gallery as his wife collapsed to the floor.

On a related note, the judge recommended that a regulatory body should be established to oversee the regulation of all writers and to ensure that the use of pennames is made illegal. He reasoned that authors should be held to account for their literary output. With that, Judge Charlie looked back to Sebastian. "You have ruined your future young man!" he said tauntingly, and then signalled to the police to take him away.

Sebastian tried to run over to his parents, but a police officer grabbed hold of his sweatshirt, preventing his escape.

"Let me go!" he cried out in anguish as he was pulled along.

Icy hail was falling as two police officers walked Sebastian through the compound at the back of the courthouse and towards an armoured prison van. The officers opened the back doors and shoved Sebastian inside. Then the engine roared to life and the vehicle began to jerk forward.

Sebastian could hear the sound of sirens as the van drove out of the compound and onto the main road. He stood on his tiptoes and looked out of the tinted glass windows. Through the sheets of hail, he could see a huge crowd of shabbily-dressed people lining the streets. Their dirty faces were contorted in expressions of hatred and they were shaking their clenched fists in the air. Members of the crowd clambered over each other, wide-eyed and foaming at the mouth, desperately trying to reach the van.

"Bigot!"

"Fanatic!"

"Extremist!" they shrieked as it drove past.

Every now and then there were loud thuds as objects thrown by the multitude hit the side of the vehicle. Sometimes crazed paparazzo would thrust their cameras up against the van's windows, all the while shouting obscenities at Sebastian. But the prison van continued steadily on its journey through the rubbish-laden streets, rocking back and forth as it drove over mounds of discarded waste. Sebastian crouched down and put his head in his hands, yearning for his parents. He said a prayer and trembled as he wondered about the fate that awaited him. Eventually the van reached its destination and shuddered to a halt. There was a scratching sound as the huge reinforced metal gates were pulled opened. Sebastian peered out again through the van's windows. 'Rehabilitation Centre' it said in large black lettering on the wall of the fortified structure they were entering.

CHAPTER 11

Sebastian once more heard the screeching of the huge metal gates closing behind him, and then the van came to a complete stop. The doors sprung open and two burly rehabilitation centre staff dragged him outside. Security guards high up on watchtowers stared down at him. Sebastian could still hear the hysterical screams of the baying mob outside the centre's perimeter fence. Security staff wearing bullet-proof vests were everywhere, aiming their assault rifles at him at all times. They marched him in through the front door of the rehabilitation centre's main building and hauled him through the sterile corridors. Adrenaline surged through Sebastian's body, making the experience take on a surreal quality. Eventually they stopped outside an office door. The guards released him from their grasp, and told him to go inside. Sebastian gulped nervously and knocked gently on the door.

"Come in!" a woman's voice said. He slowly pushed the door open and peeked inside. A middle-aged woman wearing a nurse's uniform was standing in the office. She had medium-length brown hair and a big smile on her face. In her hands, she held a cardboard folder containing a file on her new client. "Hello, I'm Nurse Harriet," she said.

The nurse leaned down and gave Sebastian an affectionate little pinch on the cheek. "We've been expecting you," she told him. Nurse Harriet had a friendly demeanour that immediately put Sebastian at ease. "You must be exhausted after everything you've been through," she said.

"Yes, a little," he replied.

Nurse Harriet told Sebastian that she was the staff member assigned to look after him during his stay at the centre, and then began to look through his file. "Oh, you have mental problems, you poor little thing!" she said. "But don't worry, we have a stockpile of your medication here," she added, handing him two pills and pouring a glass of water. After he had taken the pills, the nurse inspected the inside of his mouth to make sure he had swallowed them.

"When can I see my parents?" Sebastian asked.

Nurse Harriet looked at him sadly. "Visitors aren't allowed in the rehabilitation centre for health and safety reasons, I'm afraid," she said.

"I see..." said Sebastian, feeling distraught that his parents wouldn't be allowed to visit him.

Nurse Harriet crouched down beside him. "But I will be having regular meetings with them to let them know how you are getting on," she said. "And I will also record video messages from them for you to watch. Every Thursday at 7.00p.m., all the inmates gather in the centre's auditorium to watch video messages from loved ones."

"Umm, okay," Sebastian responded, still upset that he wouldn't be able to see his parents in person. He began to weep and Nurse Harriet gave him a big hug.

"But anyway, you have a lot of work to do today," she continued. "The harder you work, the sooner you'll be released."

"Really?" Sebastian asked as he stopped crying momentarily.

"Yes, that's how it works here." With that, the nurse took Sebastian by the hand and led him down the corridor and into an enormous work hall. The hall contained dozens and dozens of work-benches, each with its own computer. At the back wall was a big set of wooden double-doors. 'Bookbinding Room' read the metal lettering that arched over the doorway. Hundreds of men and women were sitting at work benches, typing on computers, while nurses wandered around, attending to their needs. Dozens of security staff paced back and forth along the work hall's walls.

"Are they all prisoners?" Sebastian asked, pointing to the figures working on the computers. Nurse Harriet smiled and told him to "just think of yourself and your comrades as guests".

Sebastian mulled over what she had just said. "Well, if I am a guest, am I free to leave whenever I like?"

"No" came the reply.

She led Sebastian over to a free bench by the window and told him to sit down. By now, the medication he had taken was beginning to kick in and he was feeling relaxed. Sebastian looked at the computer screen and some text appeared: "In a moment you will see a video clip of a child who will teach you an important moral lesson. Please write a short story to demonstrate that you have understood the moral lesson." Then the clip began to play. Sebastian put on the set of headphones that were attached to the computer so that he could hear the audio. A young boy, probably even younger than Sebastian, appeared and began to talk about why women sometimes aren't hired for jobs. He then went on to explain what could be done about this injustice. Sebastian felt humiliated at receiving a lecture about morals from another child, but nevertheless felt obliged to complete the task.

The boy spoke for about half a minute, and when the clip was finished, Sebastian opened the computer's word processor and started typing. He titled the story *Joan the Job Seeker.*

> *Joan had had enough of working in her current job. She didn't like the way her boss was always pestering her to do some work. So she decided that she would get a new job. One morning, she barged into her boss's office and declared "I am applying for a new job. If you don't give me a good reference I will let everybody know that you have been pestering me!" Joan's boss immediately took out a pen and paper and wrote her an excellent reference.*

Nurse Harriet looked down at the computer screen and began to read the story to herself. Her face looked serious and intense at first, as her lips mumbled silently. But her expression began to soften as she reached the end. "Well done Sebastian!" she finally said. "That is an excellent story." She told him that he needed to save it, and helped guide the cursor to the 'save' icon on the screen.

"What happens now?" Sebastian asked. Nurse Harriet informed him that the best stories written by the inmates were printed off and bound into *Moral Stories for Kids* schoolbooks that are dispatched to all the schools in the country. Sebastian felt his heart skip a beat. Even in his medicated state he was so struck by the revelation that he almost fainted. "New editions of the book are produced each year, and we want to make sure each edition contains newer and better stories than the last – all to help make the world a fairer, more equal and inclusive place for everyone!" the nurse said.

Moments later, two female inmates seated across the other side of the work hall started bickering loudly, shouting insults at each other. "I'm going to smash your head in!" one of them screeched hysterically as she jumped out of her seat and rushed towards her comrade. A security man intervened and attempted to calm the situation, but the angry woman squared up to him. "You're not the boss of me!" she shouted.

"But anyway, you'll need to write plenty more stories before the day is done," Nurse Harriet continued, looking back to Sebastian. "So, back to work!" she said jollily as she headed off to attend to other inmates.

Sebastian collected himself and tried his best to think rationally. He knew that if he was to get an early release from the rehabilitation centre he would have to be seen to be cooperative. And so he watched some more videos and listened carefully as schoolchildren explained the true causes of social ills such as crime, poverty, addiction, and discrimination. He carefully wrote a story after each viewing, pretending to approve of the moral sentiment of each lesson. For lunch, the nurses went around to each inmate and gave them a carton of milk and some sandwiches, but encouraged them to continue working while they ate.

When four o'clock came, all the inmates made their way to the centre's dining area, and a handful went into the kitchen to cook dinner. Sebastian tried to converse with some of them, but they all seemed a bit grumpy. Nurse Harriet appeared on the scene and told Sebastian that he should give a hand with the preparation. And so he went into the kitchens and started churning butter, while other inmates got to work cooking salmon, beef, roast potatoes, soup and vegetables, baking bread, pouring glasses of champagne and preparing dishes of caviar. Everything smelled delicious.

When all the food was cooked and prepared, the kitchen doors opened and several staff members entered, pushing metal trollies. They loaded all the food and drink onto them and then made their way back out of the kitchen and off down the corridor.

"Where are they taking all the food?" Sebastian asked. "I thought we were going to eat now!"

The other inmates informed him as a health and safety procedure, the staff tests all the food and drink first, to make sure that it is safe to eat. Everyone waited and waited, their stomach's groaning. After about an hour, the staff members rolled the trolleys back into the kitchen.

All that was left were potatoes, soup, and some bread and butter. All the meat, fish, champagne and caviar was gone.

The staff declared that all the food had been thoroughly tested and was edible.

"This is absolutely ridiculous" Sebastian stated aloud. "They've eaten all the best food."

The other inmates began to give Sebastian filthy looks. "You're a right troublemaker, aren't you?" one man shouted, and Sebastian could feel his spit land on his face.

"You need to learn how to share!" said another inmate. "And anyway, we could all die of food poisoning if the staff didn't test the food first."

All the inmates sat down at the tables in the dining area and the staff nurses gave them their medication. It turned out that all the inmates suffered from mental problems. Those who hadn't been diagnosed before coming to the rehabilitation centre were diagnosed by one of the nurses shortly after they arrived.

Once everyone had taken their pills, they began helping themselves to the food. Each inmate was carefully monitored by his/her comrades to make sure that they didn't take any more than anyone else. During their meal, the inmates talked about how much they hated posh people, capitalists, conservative-types and people who discriminate against others. Sebastian kept his head down and said nothing. When dinner was over, Sebastian still felt hungry and resorted to discretely scavenging little morsels of food that had fallen on the dining room's floor.

Thereafter, it was time for everyone to get back to work. The inmates headed back to the work hall to continue writing stories. Every now and then, Nurse Harriet would check how

Sebastian was getting on and review what he had written. Sebastian and his comrades worked into the night, and it was almost 12 o'clock before they were allowed go to bed. By then Sebastian was exhausted and could barely keep his eyes open. The nurses and inmates trudged down the corridor together and into a huge dormitory. There were hundreds of beds, and powerful fluorescent lights on the ceiling shone intensely, illuminating the room in a bright glow. The walls were painted a deep blue and decorated with little yellow stars. All the inmates started getting undressed and climbing into the beds, and nurses went around tucking everyone in.

"You can sleep there," Nurse Harriet said, pointing to an empty bed.

Sebastian took off his jeans and sweatshirt and climbed in. The nurse pulled the sheets over him and fixed his pillow.

"Please will you let my parents come and visit me?" Sebastian asked her once more, beginning to well up with tears again.

"I'm really sorry, but rules are rules," she replied sympathetically.

"See you in the morning," Nurse Harriet said before making her way back to her office. Sebastian closed his eyes, and although he was tired, he found it difficult to sleep under the glow of the fluorescent lights. To make matters worse, the inmate in the bed beside him started snoring loudly. Sebastian put his fingers into his ears to block out the sound, but to no avail. He twisted and turned in the bed for hours, and kept thinking about his parents. Eventually he fell into an uneasy sleep.

* * *

He awoke at 7.30a.m. when an alarm buzzer began to sound, indicating that it was time for everyone to get up. All around him, inmates started getting out of bed, but Sebastian still felt exhausted. He hadn't slept well and felt groggy. So he pulled the blankets back up over him and closed his eyes.

"What the hell are you doing!?" a voice suddenly screamed.

Sebastian looked up and saw an inmate standing by his bed. "I barely slept and I'm still tired – I'm just trying to rest," he replied.

"Get up! Get up!" the man shouted. All the other inmates began to gather around Sebastian's bed.

"If we don't get to have a lie-in then why the hell should you?" one of them yelled. They pulled the blankets off him and started dragging him from the bed. Sebastian agreed to get up, and pleaded for them to leave him alone.

After everyone had used the bathroom and taken a shower, they got dressed and headed for the dining room for breakfast. As they all made their way down the corridor, Sebastian saw Nurse Harriet approaching. "How did you sleep Sebastian?" she asked, pulling him to one side.

"Not very well, I'm afraid," he replied. "Would it be possible to turn off the lights in the bedroom at night-time, so it will be easier to sleep?" he asked.

"Of course not!" Nurse Harriet declared. She told him that the lights were always left on for health and safety reasons. "We wouldn't want someone to have a nasty fall in the dark, would we?"

So Sebastian asked if he could have a bedroom to himself. But the nurse was clearly shocked by the question. She asked Sebastian if he had anything to hide, or if he thought he was more important than everybody else. Sebastian replied that he did not. "Then why on earth would you need a bedroom all to yourself? That would just be selfish, wouldn't it?"

Sebastian thought for a moment. "I suppose it would…" he acknowledged. He began to ask Nurse Harriet once again if she would let his parents come to visit him, but she immediately shook her head from side to side. "Then can I telephone or write a letter to my best friend Adam—"

"*Best* friend?" Nurse Harriett asked, a look of disgust appearing fleetingly on her face. "People shouldn't have best friends. It makes other people feel excluded. So no, I'm afraid you won't be allowed any contact with him," she said as she shooed Sebastian back towards the other inmates who were heading to the dining room for breakfast.

As Sebastian continued along the corridor, he noticed some picture frames hanging on the wall and stopped momentarily to have look. There were four portraits of gloomy-looking old men, with grey complexions and expressionless faces. Information provided under each picture stated that they were Mr Junkers, Mr Barosa, Mr Schultz and Mr Van Herman; the board of directors who oversaw the running of the centre. Beside their pictures was another frame that contained a gold medallion, and a metal plaque indicated that it was the award that the centre had won for its excellent work rehabilitating criminals.

"Move along!" the inmates standing behind Sebastian shouted.

A group of inmates went into the kitchen to make breakfast, while the rest took their seats in the dining room. Soon the air was filled with the aromas of French toast, tea, coffee, eggs, sausages and bacon. When everything was cooked and prepared, some members of staff came along and loaded all the food and drinks onto metal trollies and began wheeling them off down the corridor. "But they'll eat all the best food..." Sebastian grumbled under his breath.

Sure enough, when the staff eventually returned with the trollies, there was only some cold tea and toast left. The inmates began helping themselves, and it was again ensured that no one took any more food or drink than anyone else. Sebastian decided he might as well try and engage in a bit of conversation with his comrades. He wanted to see if anyone else disapproved with the morals they were being taught, but knew he would need to broach the subject delicately. "Aren't some of the morals in the videos very strange?" he asked casually, trying to make it sound like a throw-away comment. Everybody at his table fell silent. "The moral lesson in a video I watched yesterday implied that the best thing to do when somebody says something that you disagree with is to shout the person down. Isn't that silly?!" he continued with a slight laugh.

"Shut the f#ck up!" a man screamed, standing up and pointing his finger at Sebastian. So angry was the man that Sebastian thought he was going to punch him.

"Don't cause trouble, Sebastian!" he suddenly heard a voice behind him say.

He turned around to see Nurse Harriet and other nurses approaching, carrying cardboard boxes full of medication. Everyone took their pills, and a few minutes later Sebastian was feeling muzzy. When breakfast was finished and all the dishes were cleared, the inmates began to shuffle back down the corridor and into the work hall. Sebastian spent the morning and afternoon watching videos of children lecturing about morals and then writing corresponding stories. During dinner, he kept his eyes directed downwards, and dared not talk to anybody. In bed that night, he again found it hard to sleep under the bright lights and with inmates snoring all around him. He pulled the blankets up over his head and cried himself to sleep.

* * *

The days passed, but Sebastian struggled to adapt to life at the rehabilitation centre. He found it difficult to get along with the other inmates. They were rude and obnoxious, but also hypersensitive about anybody offending them. This inevitably led to many shouting matches between them and even occasional physical altercations. On the rare occasions Sebastian dared question the moral lessons taught by the schoolchildren or the numerous health and safety measures at the centre, they got angry with him. And so he quickly learned to keep his opinions to himself. All the same, he worked as hard as he could and always took his medication without protest.

Nurse Harriet organised for some children's trousers, tracksuits, t-shirts, hoodies and shoes to be sent to the centre's laundry, so that Sebastian could have a fresh set of clothes every day. He continued to beg her to bend the rules and let his mummy and daddy pay him a visit, but the nurse kept telling him that this wasn't possible. However, she told him that she herself would shortly pay them a visit, and record a message from them.

* * *

And so, early on Thursday morning, while all the inmates were writing stories, Nurse Harriet made her way out through the rehabilitation centre's front door and headed for her car, which was parked in the staff car park. She drove out through the huge metal gates at the entrance to the compound, waved on by security. Once outside, Nurse Harriet locked her car's doors and avoided eye contact with pedestrians and other motorists as she drove through the grimy city streets. The car bounced along the pothole-covered roads, but Nurse Harriet didn't flinch. Eventually she arrived at the new high-rise apartment complex where Sebastian's parents were now living.

She parked her car and walked up the urine-stained concrete stairwell, scurrying past the gangs of youths loitering in the corridors. She located the Howards' apartment and knocked at the door. The door creaked open slightly, as much as the secured bolt chain would allow.

"Who is it?" Sebastian's father asked in a hushed tone.

"It's Nurse Harriet from the rehabilitation centre. I'm here to talk to you about Sebastian."

Mr Howard quickly undid the chain and invited the nurse to come in. "Sorry about that. We have a lot of problems around here with hooliganism," he said.

"I actually feel very sorry for hooligans," Nurse Harriet replied. "As everyone knows, they're a very much discriminated-against group."

Mr Howard led the nurse into the main room in the apartment and invited her to sit down on the sofa, but she said she'd rather stand by the window so she could admire the beauty of the cityscape. Sebastian's mother offered the nurse a cup of tea, which she gladly accepted.

"Sebastian isn't making much progress at all," Nurse Harriet began. "He's been at the centre for almost a week now, but isn't very cooperative and doesn't work nearly hard enough." Sebastian's parents looked at each other, surprised by this revelation.

"Sebastian normally works so hard at home…" they said.

Nurse Harriet went on to tell the couple that the harder their son worked, the sooner he would be released. "So we will need to somehow motivate him. At the pace he's working now, he will almost certainly have to serve the full 25 years of his sentence," she said, putting her hand up to her chin. Mr Howard questioned Nurse Harriet about the nature of the work Sebastian was doing in the rehabilitation centre, but the nurse was evasive and just gave vague answers.

Nurse Harriet glanced down at her car in the parking lot to make sure it wasn't being vandalised, and then continued. "I haven't said anything to Sebastian about his poor work ethic, as it might hurt his feelings." She went on to explain that while visitors weren't allowed in the rehabilitation centre, she could record a message from them for their son to view. With that, she took a small handheld video camera out of her uniform pocket and pointed it at the couple. Mr and Mrs Howard began to speak, and when they were done, Nurse Harriet put the camera back in her pocket and headed for the door. Sebastian's broken-hearted parents remained distraught about their son's arrest and imprisonment, but were slightly relieved by the news that he might be released early if he worked hard. They thanked the nurse for all her help as she left. Nurse Harriet returned to her car and headed off to visit some other inmates' families.

When she arrived back at the rehabilitation centre that afternoon, she went straight to her office and loaded all the videos she had recorded into the software editing programme on her computer. She edited out any extraneous or otherwise unnecessary information, and then uploaded them to them centre's cinema system. She then went into the work hall to see how the inmates were getting on.

Sebastian had taken a moment away from his work and was leaning on the windowsill, gazing out the window. He could see building work underway in the rehabilitation centre's compound and stood on his tiptoes to get a better look. Behind a thick concrete wall, hordes of workers were constructing beautiful villas. Each villa had a swimming pool in the back garden and some even had tennis courts. A cobblestoned pathway ran past the villas and led up to a red-bricked school building. In through the school's windows, Sebastian could see classrooms containing microscopes, globes, abacuses and geographical maps. The surrounding gardens were full of immaculately-trimmed hedges, flowerbeds and fountains.

Nurse Harriet went over to him to see what he was looking at, and Sebastian pointed over towards the villas that were being constructed and asked if all the inmates would move into them when they were completed. But Nurse Harriet told him that that area was exclusively for the rehabilitation centre staff and their families. With that, she gently pulled him away from the window.

"You'd better get back to work now," she said.

The day progressed as usual, and at seven o'clock, it was time for the weekly viewing of messages from family members. Sebastian trudged along with his comrades to the auditorium and took a seat. Soon the room was packed, and as there were more people than seats, many inmates stood in the aisles. In the darkness, Sebastian could see a huge cinema screen adhered to the wall. The fourth movement of Beethoven's *Ninth Symphony* played softly on the auditorium's sound system. The music slowly faded away and the cinema screen lit up. A clip began to play of a woman and two little girls sitting in a living room. Sebastian didn't recognise them, but from what he gathered they were the wife and daughters of another new inmate.

As the woman began to speak, most inmates began to laugh and jeer. The girls proceeded to say how much they missed their daddy, and his wife encouraged him to work very hard so that he might be released early. The other inmates pointed at the man for whom the video message was intended and hurled insults and him. "Aww, he loves his wife and kids! What an idiot!" they shouted mockingly. Within seconds, the man was in tears. When the clip had finished playing, Sebastian's parents appeared on the cinema screen. As they began to speak, the other inmates again began to laugh and sneer. Sebastian could feel everyone's eyes focused on him, but he managed to hold back his tears. "The little baby misses his mummy and daddy!" they laughed.

He looked around and saw several nurses, including Nurse Harriet, standing in the shadows at the back of the auditorium, but they did nothing to stop the fiasco. But Sebastian listened intently, trying to hear what his parents were saying. They told him that they loved him very much, but instructed him to work much, much harder. When they had finished speaking, videos for other inmates started to play. Sebastian was glad that the focus was now off of him, and greatly relieved that his parents were safe and well.

In total, 24 video clips played, one for each of the newer detainees. For the entire duration of the session in the auditorium, most inmates laughed and jeered when each clip played. "*This is horrendous…*" Sebastian thought. It was almost 8.00p.m. by the time everyone left the auditorium. Sebastian tried to converse with some of the other new inmates as they walked back down the corridor together, but Nurse Harriet kept butting in.

Soon everyone was back in the work hall writing stories. Sebastian looked out of the work hall window and saw all the lights go out across the city. He continued working away, and when midnight eventually came he and all the other inmates were exhausted. Everyone headed back to the dormitory and went to bed.

* * *

As the weeks went by, Sebastian gradually fell into the daily routine of life in the rehabilitation centre. It was a tough existence, as he was required to work seven days a week, and the only opportunities to rest were during meal times, when watching videos in the auditorium, and in bed at night. However, as Sebastian came to realise, most inmates didn't actually work too hard anyway. They spent much of their time quarrelling with each other (as well as with the centre's staff), daydreaming or staring out the window.

The centre grew busier each week as more and more new inmates began serving their sentences. To make sure that the inmates didn't feel excluded from the rest of society, the staff began to bring them copies of a daily newspaper to read. The paper was always filled with good news about how delightful life was in the nation.

When looking out the work hall window, Sebastian would sometimes see the centre's board members, Mr Junkers, Mr Schultz, Mr Barosa and Mr Van Herman, walking around by the villas in the staff quarters, playing tennis or swimming. Although they seemed to be enjoying themselves, they always looked a bit dull, and unlike Nurse Harriet and the other nurses, they never made any effort to interact with the inmates.

Nurse Harriet was always on hand to help Sebastian with any problems he encountered, and also had regular meetings with his parents to keep them up to date with his progress and record their messages. She continued to express to them her concerns that Sebastian wasn't working hard enough, and that if they couldn't somehow manage to motivate him, he might have to serve his full sentence.

Although he found his duties boring and monotonous, Sebastian worked diligently in the work hall, writing short stories to complement the moral values taught to him by the children in the videos. He sometimes helped prepare the food for breakfast and dinner, and at seven o'clock each Thursday evening, he went to the auditorium to watch video messages sent to the newer inmates from their families. He tried his best to ignore the taunts of his comrades as he watched the messages from his parents, who invariably begged him to work harder.

* * *

Eventually, Sebastian's birthday arrived. However, despite the joyous occasion, he was moody that morning. The day began badly when he told some other inmates that it was his birthday and they replied, "So bloody what?" Also, the poor quality sleep he got each night under the fluorescent lights, combined with poor diet, the effects of his medication and the general lack of privacy in the rehabilitation centre had him feeling grouchy. And his parents' constant demands for him to work harder were also getting on his nerves.

Sebastian had been writing stories all morning, and when he paid a brief visit to the work hall's unisex toilet, Nurse Harriet started pounding on the cubicle door. "Come out quickly Sebastian. There's a delivery for you!" she said.

Nurse Harriet led Sebastian into to her office, and there, sitting on her desk, was a parcel wrapped in yellow paper and purple ribbon. A sealed envelope lay on top. Sebastian excitedly tore open the envelope and pulled out a card. It was from his parents.

> *Happy Birthday Sebastian! Due to financial difficulties, we couldn't afford to buy you a new gift, but sent along one of your favourite books instead. Lots of Love, from Mummy and Daddy.*
>
> *P.S. We miss you so much. Please work harder so you can come home soon.*

Sebastian sighed. "How much harder do they expect me to work?" he muttered.

"Oh, your parents are very hard on you," Nurse Harriet said solemnly. "I can't understand why they keep badgering you to work harder. Every time I meet them I keep telling them that I think you work *extremely* hard. I bet your daddy is especially mean to you isn't he?" she asked.

"Yes!" Sebastian replied. "One time when he was in bad mood he told me that my bedroom looked like a pigsty, and another time he yelled at me just because I wandered around the city by myself after dark."

"That's terrible!" the nurse exclaimed, putting her hands up to her cheeks. "Well, don't worry. I will tell the centre's directors what a diligent little worker you are, and hopefully we can get you released early."

"Thank you," Sebastian replied as he picked up his gift and tore off the wrapping paper. It was *The Big Book of Puzzles: Critical Thinking Extravaganza!* that Adam had bought him for his previous birthday.

Nurse Harriet eyed the book suspiciously. "Hmm, it's a book of puzzles…" she said dispassionately. She yanked the book from Sebastian's hands and began to look through the colourful images inside. "Here's a nice animal puzzle! Try this one Sebastian," she said, handing the book back to him. There were five illustrations of different animals: a horse, a dog, a cat, a goldfish, and a rabbit. At the bottom of the page, the text read "Which is the odd one out?"

Sebastian stared down at the animals but the answer wasn't coming to him.

"So?" Nurse Harriet asked after a few seconds, encouraging him to respond.

"Well…" said Sebastian. "I think the odd one out is the horse. He's the biggest, so he probably bullies all the other animals."

"Oh yes, that's an excellent answer!" the nurse replied. She asked him if he wanted to try another one, but he said he didn't as he had a headache now from all the thinking.

"You poor thing," she responded in a sympathetic tone. "I don't know why your mummy and daddy would send you a present that just gives you a headache."

"Nor do I," Sebastian replied.

Sebastian tucked the card into the book and headed back to the work hall. "Look everybody, Sebastian has a book!" one of the other inmates shouted. The man grabbed it out from under Sebastian's arm began to read through it. "Hmm, these puzzles are very difficult," he said before handing it to someone else. Soon the book was being passed around and before long it disappeared out of Sebastian's sight. He didn't mind though, because he knew that sharing his gift was the morally correct thing to do.

Sebastian sat back down at his work bench, put on the headphones and watched another video. He tried his best to stay focused as a little girl explained the real reason parents discipline their kids, and what children could do about such mistreatment. When the clip was finished, Sebastian began to write a story called *Mary the Strict Mother*.

Mary was very strict with her son, which made her feel powerful and important. "But I want to play my computer games!" her son would say as she incessantly asked him to do some chores around the house. This scenario played out day after day, until eventually the little boy screamed at his mother. "If you don't let me play my computer games I will report you to social services!"

Mary never bothered her son about doing chores again.

After dinner, Sebastian went in search of the birthday gift from his parents. He asked several of the other inmates if they knew where it was, but none of them did. He searched in the kitchen and in the dormitory, but it was nowhere to be found. Eventually he located it lying on the floor in the toilet. Its spine was broken and numerous pages were torn out. The card lay nearby and was in an even more sorry state. It was crumpled up and one of the other inmates had apparently used it as toilet paper. As the book and card seemed to be beyond repair, Sebastian threw them in the bin.

* * *

The months ticked by and Sebastian had noticed that it was taking him longer and longer to complete stories because his attention span wasn't quite what it used to be. He could only stay focused for a few seconds at a time, and would often be distracted by what was happening out of the work hall window. He could see that the city outside had become very dilapidated. Many of the beautiful old buildings which had once graced the city's skyline had fallen into ruin, while others had been demolished and replaced by high-rise concrete tower blocks.

At night, nightmares began to flood Sebastian's mind. He kept thinking of all the upset that he had caused everyone with his crime involving the counterfeit schoolbooks. A deep sense of shame came over him, but he became resolved to change his ways and turn over a new leaf. And so he worked hard, day after day, week after week. Sometimes he would be instructed to work in the bookbinding room, where he would operate one of the numerous electronic printing presses, printing off copies of moral stories and then binding them into schoolbooks. He would then help pack the finished products into wooden crates so they could be transported to all the schools in the country in time for the next academic school term. Over time, Sebastian began to feel a sense of contentment knowing that he was playing his part in helping to instil good moral values in little children.

* * *

One afternoon while in the work-hall, once again distracted, Sebastian wandered over to the window and leaned on the windowsill. He looked over towards an area of scrubland within the centre's compound where he could see industrial vehicles and inmates digging holes in the earth. Working in pairs, a group of inmates were unloading objects wrapped in white sheets from the back of a lorry. The objects sagged downwards in the middle as the men carried them over to a pit and tossed them in. A man was standing before the inmates, brandishing a crop and shouting commands at them. Sebastian looked closely and saw that it was Mr

Wallace! When a pit was full the vehicles covered it over with soil and clay and then drove over the remaining mound, smoothing it down.

Sebastian called Nurse Harriet over and pointed towards where Mr Wallace was standing. "That man used to be my school's head teacher," he said.

"I know," Nurse Harriet responded. "He works here in the rehabilitation centre now. He's very nice, isn't he?"

"Yeah, he's alright, I guess," Sebastian replied. He asked her what Mr Wallace and the inmates were doing, and she told him that they were just disposing of some rubbish.

"Come on Sebastian, back to work!" Nurse Harriet then said cheerfully, clapping her hands.

"Alright, alright!" Sebastian barked at her.

* * *

By the autumn, Sebastian's demeanour had become increasingly like that of the other inmates. He was irritable all the time and would fly off the handle whenever someone caused him even the slightest offence. But he continued to work hard, trying his best to stay focused on writing stories and doing any other tasks that Nurse Harriet requested of him. And once a week he sat in the auditorium with the other inmates and viewed messages from his parents. He also kept up-to-date with current affairs through the newspapers, and learnt that the private ownership of property and all private commerce had been made illegal (this law had in fact been enacted across most of Europe).

One Thursday evening, at seven o'clock, Sebastian sauntered down the hallway in an irritable daze and joined the rest of the inmates in the auditorium. He sat down and leaned back in the seat. It felt good to have a rest, even if just for a few minutes. Videos messages for the inmates began to play, and as usual, the auditorium erupted into the sound of jeers and heckles. Eventually, Sebastian's parents appeared on the screen. Sebastian noticed that they looked haggard and gaunt, and his father was unshaven. "We want to tell you that we love you very much Sebastian, but we want you to work *much* harder," Mrs Howard said.

As the inevitable roar of laughter began, something in Sebastian's head snapped. He leaped out of his seat and darted across the auditorium, towards the huge screen. He pummelled on it violently with his fists and tried to rip it apart. A shower of blue sparks erupted from cinema system and after a few seconds the image of his parents flickered and then the transmission went dead. The auditorium was silent for a few seconds. Sebastian's face was bright red and his eyes were bulging. "I never want to see them again!" he screamed, pointing at the damaged cinema screen. All the other inmates started to clap.

"Go on Sebastian! You're the man!" they shouted. "Don't let your parents push you around."

"I'm so sick of my mummy and daddy always trying to force me to work harder!" Sebastian roared.

Nurse Harriet rushed over and crouched down beside him. "Well, don't worry," she said softly. "You will never have to see them again if you don't want to."

"I don't!" Sebastian screamed.

Nurse Harriet's face beamed. "No matter how hard you work they will never be satisfied," she said, wincing into space.

As technicians began to fix the broken cinema screen, all the inmates went back to the work hall. Sebastian sat down at his bench adjacent to the window. He was gradually creating a new story on his computer. Every few seconds he would glance out of the work hall window, and when he was looking in the direction of the staff living quarters, he noticed Mr Wallace walk out onto the balcony of one of the villas. He stood there with his chest out and shoulders back, looking powerful and important as he stared out over the crumbling city. Then he sat down at a table, positioned in the late evening sunshine, poured himself a glass of champagne and tucked into a dish of caviar. Sebastian waved over to him but Mr Wallace was too engrossed in his meal to notice.

* * *

The years rolled by, and Sebastian gained a reputation for being a somewhat diligent worker who occasionally completed duties on time and who always made a special effort to ensure that every story he wrote carried an important moral lesson. As his mental health continued to improve, he was gradually weaned off his medication until eventually he no longer needed to take it at all. Although he continued to maintain a reasonably good relationship with Nurse Harriet, he would sometimes verbally abuse her when she got on his nerves. But she never gave out or punished him.

Like most inmates who had been in the rehabilitation centre a considerable time, Sebastian had long ago decided that he no longer wished to receive messages from his own family. But nevertheless, every Thursday he would sit in the auditorium and dutifully join in the heckling and jeering of new inmates as they watched video messages from their family members, to help break the bond between them. "*Why should they love their spouses and kids more than they love anybody else*?" he would think to himself. At eight o'clock each evening he would look out of the work hall window and watch all the lights in the city disappear as the electricity was switched off. On clear nights, a beautiful canopy of twinkling stars would illuminate the night sky. Sebastian noticed that one star shone slightly brighter than the others, and then he realised that it was a planet. But he couldn't remember its name.

* * *

One evening, Nurse Harriet, now old and grey, and some other staff members came over to Sebastian and gathered around him as he worked. They told him that they were very happy with his progress and that he was now completely cured of his mental problems. They all smiled as they informed him that he would be released in the morning. Nurse Harriet chatted with Sebastian for a while over green tea and organic biscuits, reminiscing about the 20 years she had worked with him, helping to make him better (satisfied that he was now fully rehabilitated, the centre's board of directors allowed him five years off his sentence). She told him that the world outside had changed a lot during his stay in the rehabilitation centre, but assured him that he needn't worry because it was wonderful out there now. Everybody got along with everybody else and all were fully included.

When Nurse Harriet left, Sebastian sat back down at his work bench. He would only have time to write one more story. So he turned to his computer and thought for a moment. He would call this story *Sebastian the Troublemaker*. He opened a blank document on the word processor and began to type.

> *Sebastian was a very selfish little boy whose snobby mummy and daddy were married to each other. He wouldn't share everything he had with the other boys and girls, which made them so upset they became burglars and thieves...*

Sebastian worked long into the night writing and redrafting the story until it was perfect. He made sure to save it so that copies could be printed off and bound into schoolbooks, which would be distributed throughout all the nation's schools. He started to drift off momentarily as tiredness weighed down his eyelids. Suddenly a clock chimed, bringing him back to his senses. Sebastian peered out of the work hall window and looked over the rehabilitation centre's barbed-wire perimeter fence and through the blanket of fog, which shrouded the city. Off in the distance he could see the faint moonlit outline of Big Ben, which had just struck 12 o'clock. It was time for bed. Tomorrow he would be released and would go and live in freedom with everybody else, in a world of equality, diversity and inclusion.

Lightning Source UK Ltd.
Milton Keynes UK
UKOW04f1904170315

248065UK00004B/369/P